Moonfall

Moonfall

Heather Spears

A Tesseract Book
Beach Holme Publishers Limited
Victoria, B.C.

Copyright © 1991 Heather Spears

This edition is published by Beach Holme Publishers Limited, 4252 Commerce Circle, Victoria, B.C., V8Z 4M2, with the assistance of the Canada Council and the B.C. Ministry of Municipal Affairs, Recreation and Culture. This is a Tesseract Book.

Cover design by Gerald Luxton.
Edited by: Gerry Truscott.
Production editor: Cheryl Smiley.

Candian Cataloguing in Publication Data

Spears, Heather, 1934—
    Moonfall

    ISBN 0-88878-306-X

    I. Title.
PS8537.P42M6 1991   C813'.54   C91-091561-X
PR9199.3.S63M6 1991

for Daniel

The author wishes to thank Göran Sonnevi for permission to reprint and translate the last four stanzas of his poem (without title): "Tankarna är också färger" from *Ditker utan ordning*, (Stockholm: Bonniers, 1983), pp. 104-105.

one

1

Tasman's earliest memories were not good ones. A brightness not escapable—she is lying in a transparent box and being watched. Also touched. She is also crawling about in it—the memories were not really that early, for her life up to the age of four was punctuated by these periods in the box—and the faces of the watchers, large and oval, behind the transparent walls that are rather moist, slippery, and warm. Two faces that return, prevail: these are the faces of her mothers, they carry over to the times at home, which seemed to her to have always been toward Kaamos, in the Darkening of the year, shadowy. Mamel's face, the large oval swimming on the right, gentle, the eyes not always ready to meet hers, looking askance, up and away as if asking for help. Mamar's on the left, a mirror likeness but something firmer, the set of the mouth a little tighter, the look more steady. Their swart skin, darker than the tunic's brownish weave with its paler, sunbleached headsleeves, their coarse hair braided away from their eyebrows women-fashion (shorter then, cut at her birth). Tasman is lifted out of the box and suckled and caressed. Otherwise watched, touched by fingers, instruments. Other faces watched her. Always twinned.

She suffered, as one "suffers" an illness—and hers was an inexplicable congenital deformity—surely long before she was aware even of her ordinary physical boundaries, though she explored her motor powers—her hands were not the box or the sheets, her will extended her fingers or clasped them, her voice uttered noises that were not the clicks and bleeps of the machines, she learned by ordinary effort to grasp her feet, roll over, sit up and so on. Her handicap became evident to her not so much from her experience of her body as from the looks and touches—the anxiety and commiseration in her mothers' (in Mamar's, resignation like a continuous exhalation of breath, in Mamel's, something still complex and unfinished, as if struggling with itself). And this look or something like it but distanced, in the other faces, a curiosity that saw her as an object—and, in the faces of some who cared for her, fear. Even avoidance of touch, or a touch that was superficial and different, and no meeting of eyes.

So there was no particular moment when Tasman, growing, learning to speak and, so very precociously, to walk, became aware of what she was. In one sense she had always been aware: she saw that human communication is not always worried, or fearful, or different, or impossible to establish; she knew this by the way the adults around her communicated with each other, so that the deep twin-bond that was everywhere was learned by her through observation and exile.

> *Stronger than father, stronger than mother,*
> *Sister to sister, brother to brother*

—an innocent nursery-rhyme now, that had once been a battle-cry, in the far-off times of the Outdead. Mamar and Mamel, leaning into each others' smiles.

Her weaning was formal, but private. Knowing no better, she accepted her gifts and made the short speeches and felt in part what she ought to have felt. She was four years old, the ceremony rather early, but there was no reason to extend infancy in her case. ("She can suck only her fingers, after all.") Perhaps here, standing before her mothers, with the decorative bluish wax still tingling and cooling on her lips. She understood for the first time what it meant to have no twin to turn to. The ceremony was performed at home. The final lines were not said, or their responses. She was used to being bereft, but not this frightened.

They lived in Lofot on the Barents Sea, in a small, level house the roof of which formed most of the yard. The city lay at the foot of the long, broken plain that extended westward from the mountains, a diked city, so far north as to be cool in late Darkening, a place of sweet air and rains that laid the dust and traced hot lines on the skin, of great tides that surged against the bulwarks, and locks on the canals, where the children swam even before they could walk, and people crossed in the water as often as over the bridges.

The city was modern. She remembered it mostly in Darkening, its lights that swelled and changed colour, gradual and ordinary, through the hours. The colours through the frothy leaves, and shimmering in long vertical pathways on the canal beyond their house. She had no fathers. They had gone away, they were dead in the Savannas, stories of them were muddled in her mind with the great tales. She thought they were Travellers, because she wanted to believe this, Tellers of letters, though really they had gone away in the aftermath of her birth, escaping. Mamel told stories to her, so early that they became confused with what little she knew of her fathers, and she let it remain so. The hero Saduth Twel, whose twin was bitten in the ear by a venomous snake as he slept.

"But wasn't the Twel waking?"

"It happened so fast, Twel was looking the other way. Nothing could save the Twar and he commanded his brother, using the strong oath, to garotte him before the poison reached their lungs, and he did, using his hand-hair, and the Twar died looking into his eyes, and did not loosen it, even as he was dying.

He struggled not / against his brother:
He died and wished him life."

"Then what happened?"

"Twel felt very sick, he knew he must leave Twar and burn his mind in the desert, but he had no tools except the short knife. But he threaded the hand-hair of his brother's palm into a fine wire, and with this, and the knife, he did the act."

Tasman's hands, which were bald, moved involuntarily to her neck. "How could he live?"

"He stanched the wound, he burned the Twar mind in a basket of long grass. Twel was very sick. For two days he mourned.

'It would be better for me
To go with you into death.
Why have you wished me life?
You are content, but I am alone.'"

12

"Alone," whispered Tasman. The word was archaic, almost taboo. She shivered.

"Why do you tell her these tales?" asked Mamar in the rote speech, and received the rote answer, "Because she asks, and because they are part of our heritage."

"Did Saduth Twel live?" asked Tasman.

"He came to Whalsay, and he was crawling. They saw him from the city, moving across the valley between Whalsay and Hoy Mountain, in the open marshes. His face was black. He lived, because it was the wish of his twin. That was a long time ago."

"Who was the hero?"

"They were both heroes, but it is called the tale of the Hero Saduth Twel."

The story absorbed Tasman; she speculated about heroes, and her fathers. A snake had killed them surely, and in the real story, which corresponded with what had occurred, the Twar would not be so unkind as to wish life on his Twel, he would drag the hair-wire loose at the last minute "with both hands," his need for air stronger than his will. They would wrestle on the ground like the unweaned, yelling and biting at each others' ears and noses, the sharp crack of their skulls would resound in the desert:

> *Bad sound / worst of all,*
> *The moon will fall, the moon will fall.*

She had seen children chided with this verse, and going untouched for punishment. And she had heard this sound on the street, unmistakable, as she lay on the bushy roof and watched them playing. And once, at night—shouts outside and that awful whiplash crack, and the sound of two feet running.

And she saw the moon past the lights, or cool and seemingly smaller in the daylight sky; they said it would fall one day, it was nearing the earth. But not in this generation. Wise men not yet born would prevent this, said her mothers. There is a great Book in Manj'u, an entire city, dedicated to this learning. The moon and the earth would be friendly, there would be conversation between them in those unimaginable days, they would turn their faces to each other in kindness. There would be two worlds.

2

T asman, at her weaning, was given garments that her mothers prepared specially for her. They were the usual sleeved tunic, but only one sleeve was open to pull over her head, the other was closed with seams and stuffed with grass. Though Tasman had several of these tunics, she came to call them by one name, Pillowmarie. At four, she resisted wearing Pillowmarie furiously, but her mothers kept it on her with intricate slips tied behind her shoulders ("She might as well get used to it") and gradually she understood that her freedom outside the house was greater, going with her mothers to receive food or walking with them along the dikes was now possible, even when people were about—though there were stares, the adult looks were at least subdued and apologetic, not scared or hostile.

Her mothers were perhaps overprotective, making her wear Pillowmarie in the house. She knew they had conversations about this and quarrels, tears also, when she was supposed to be asleep. Mamel saying, "It will train her to tilt her head."

And Mamar: "Nothing will make her look normal. We believed she was a Twel mind, heart heavy, but she has not revealed it. I can't feel it."

"She's both and must be and the Twel's strongest."

Tears. "Have her, then. Twel—you were the one who couldn't bear it."

Tasman did not understand much of this. The Pillowmarie was placed on her right one day, on her left another. It was as if they were waiting for her to show a preference. The cloth flopped against her ear, interfering with her peripheral vision. Bits of straw poked out, pricked her cheek. She sensed her mothers watching. She sat by them and ate, now out of her own bowl. The bowl, a weaning gift of baked earth, was double, and she ate with whatever hand she pleased. Pillowmarie bobbed against her temple. If Mamel painted a face on Pillowmarie with wax, would it breathe or eat?

For a time, when she was about five years old, as she drowsed off to sleep in the heat of Lightening, Tasman talked to herself, almost as if she were trying to pretend she had a twin. Her hands talked, or perhaps the location of her two play personalities was in her shoulders. She chose to become the voice of one side or the other—such play was listened to and remembered by Mamar for Book. Tasman lying restless on the pallet and talking softly.

"I am going to Book.... *And-you-come-too,*" (a courtesy speech). "Then I an going to World *and-you-come-too.* Just before Kaamos, in the Darkening of the year. There is a big story in Book and I'll read it to you. Thank you. I'll draw you pictures, it will have a desert in, a Savannah. They give you colours in Book, and you can have lights. You can colour with lights. *Fire in my mind, water in your mind.* I want to "(here she whispered) "and light real fires, big ones....Aren't you afraid? I'm not afraid, I'm going to Book soon and you aren't even there."

This last was said with some defiance and satisfaction. Tasman did want to learn and had really no problem in choosing Book instead of World. World children did not have an institution, but wandered. That they were allowed to play with fire was an enormous enticement. They played with fire on the beaches and ran with the tides and touched real things. At Book, nothing was real, although, apart from the rote tales, it corresponded. The excitement was that it was seemingly endless, doors lifting to reveal more doors lifting as if forever. The children might ask anything at all and the answers prepared them for more asking. Most children went to Book, eagerly, when they were weaned, which could be at five or nine, or even later if they were male. They had played enough with the world by then, though some would choose to return to it. Weaned twins had to work out where they most wanted to go. *Real fire burns Book. Book is a fire that burns forever.* It was a lesson in cooperation, perhaps the most difficult of any they would face. Sometimes a twin at Book never learned to read, but drew endlessly while his brother read or played with numbers; the screens were doubled, set side by side. There were laboratories as well as libraries. The teachers were there to show them how to use Book, to find the answers to anything they asked.

Tasman had to wait longer than her fifth year before there was a Book that could or would take her. And that first attempt proved disastrous.

Even with Pillowmarie her appearance at Book frightened the smaller children, and the older ones were interrupted. Questions were suddenly not about subjects that had interested them before, but about Tasman; scared twins her own age clung to the teachers: "What happened to her twin?" But the older children wanted to know about the oldest tales. Tasman, meanwhile, miserable at a screen she had so looked forward to manipulating, drew aimlessly while big boys passed behind her and whispered to each other. "Let us ask to read this, it is about the Outdead." By the end of the day, no one was interested in anything else. Teachers stroked her but she felt anxiousness in their touch. She wanted to go home.

"Will you go to World, then?"

"I want Book, not World, I want Book."

And now Tasman, too, wanted to know about the barbaric Outdead, and to read the oldest tales. But no Book would take her.

3

H er mothers had received a letter she did not hear, but they spoke of it. They stopped taking her past the yard, even with Pillowmarie. It was approaching the Darkening of the year. She lay on the roof, in the heat, watching the low sun beyond the fronds, the bit of glistening sea past the dikes to the northwest.

> *"In the night of the afternoon / we will come calling. In Darkening we will touch you / where no one has touched you since your weaning."*

An old love song, high, sorrowful male voices intertwining, from a roof farther down the street. Soon the blue lights of afternoon would turn the reddish dusty air to gray, and the grass, and all the leaves and the white jasmine would be blue. Great red-black clouds hindered and released the sun as it slipped towards the sea. The moon's wind fluttered, then grew a little stronger, pushing the hot air out over the water, and she leaned forward to savour it, tucking Pillowmarie under her chin. When I learn to read, she thought, I will read the oldest tales first of all.

"Mar, tell me about the Outdead."

Mamar spoke sharply. "You will learn that at Book, we know so little."

"I want to go to Book now. Tell me what you know."

Mamel sighed. "I will tell you something—Mar can sleep if she likes." They stroked Tasman; they were lying on the pallet; she sensed it was Mamar's touch, resigned now and gentle.

"Once upon a time, there were more Outdead than people on the earth. Although they were human, they were fierce and cruel. They lived in great cities that are now ruins near in the Sheath; and it is difficult or impossible to explore those places because of the heat. But some people say that when the moon comes near, it will be cooler there and we will again traverse the earth."

"How could the Outdead live there, when it is so hot?"

"It was not so hot then, Tasman. They lived there very well."

"Did they come and kill us?"

"No, our race lived there too. At first, there were very few of us—and when we were born, they killed us if they found us. But parents also killed their own children. Every bicephalic child, for this was what they called us, was killed, it was a decree, but some were saved—in the cities in their Medical Book; they say the fathers of our race, Janus, lived to maturity because they were in Book. But there is another tale about Janus."

"Tell me."

"It was in the place called Lond, which is a great fiery ruin now on the edge of the Savannah in the peninsula. The Janus were born. Their mother was of the Outdead, a barbarian among barbarians, and she looked at them and said,

> *'This was a hard birth, and I knew | who you*
> *would be, Janus my sons. | I knew my thighs*
> */would nearly break bearing you. | My face*
> *is black. | I cannot walk, or I would hide you.'"*

So she gave then to her housebond and begged him to kill them, because she could not hide them and there were by then too many in the Medical Book; and some said, they killed them there also. Her housebond, however, took pity on them, and wrapped them up and took them into the east part of that country, and no one stopped him."

"Was it Darkening?"

Mamar spoke. "In Book, you will learn that it becomes dark and light very swiftly in the Sheath of the world."

"So he ran in the short dark," went on Mamel, "and in the short light he rested and hid. Perhaps he fed them the milk of snakes, but some say he himself made milk for them out of their importunity:

> *His nipples were two eyes | and they opened*
> */weeping for Janus."*

"I do not know how they survived. Janus' grown body fathered twins, whose mothers were much younger, they were the Effe, whom some say were only eleven years old, but perhaps they were thirteen or fourteen."

"Were the Effe hid in Book?"

"Surely, Tasman, but they were considered too young to be watched. Effe and Janus had many children while they lived.

> *Effe Twel and Effe Twar,*
> *First mothers, help us bear."*

"Were their children killed?"

"Not all. Janus had a kind of fortress city by then in the eastern peninsula. It was the time of the terrible slaughterings and mutilations. But no more Outdead were being born. I do not know why the Outdead did not learn gentleness, or surrender, but it is said that their loneliness was eating into them and they were crazed. Remember that they had powerful cities and enormous wealth. And what they prepared they could not erase, they made everything that is valuable to us—Book, and the cars, lights and many intricate serviceable devices which they would have taken with them into destruction if they could. But they had been too clever; they were unable to harm them. They lived long into our age, but they died. They preached and practiced genocide against our race. It is said, they refused to look at their own children, but had them killed. Wherever they found us, they killed us."

Tasman looked from one to the other of her mothers' faces. Mamar's gaze was steady and sad. Mamel's difficult, made ugly by eyes not yet finished with crying, mouth stretched to a tight smile. She said, "At Book, the other children asked about the Outdead when they saw you. That does not mean you have anything to do with that ancient race. You are good and kind, though your feet and hands are bald, and no one knows why you were born untwinned. You asked us about the Saduth because of this, and we told you, because it is good for you to know that being alone is possible on the earth."

They told Tasman the other tale of Janus also, and no one knows which one corresponds with what was, or whether they really lived. But they did not tell her of the mutilations (and he may have been one), most of whom did not live, because it is said that in Lond and Camp David and some of the other cities there were two and three generations who were unilater-

ally garotted, and who in turn unilaterally garotted
their infant children, and held the power like kings;
but they were overthrown. There were many old
tales, some more terrible than these.

4

O ne morning when Tasman was nearly six, she
was told that there was a Book that would take
her. "It is very small," her mothers said, as they
dressed her and knotted her hair. "It is on the out-
skirts of the city and we will take you there every day
in the cars."

"You knew about it yesterday. You heard a letter
when I was sleeping."

"Stay still. Where do you want Pillowmarie?"

"I don't care. Twel: I'm going to Book."

They did not tell her that it was an institution connected to the medical Book, and fortunately it was
beyond it, in a separate building, and going in the
closed cars Tasman would not even see the place she
disliked so much. With Pillowmarie hooded on her
left shoulder, she sat upright all the way, wary
because she could feel they were moving in the direction her body still recognized, and only easy when she
felt they had been longer on the way, though they
stopped soon enough.

When her mothers left her, and she was taken in and shown around, Tasman saw that it was indeed small. It was a long windowless room past an entrance which they had walked down into, along a new ramp of hard earth, and past big curtains that her mothers had pushed up to reveal a large, low, lighted space, mostly bare, with mats on the floor and all the furniture of the screens at the other end. And as if it were a beach, or World, small objects lay about, little rafts, bits of honed wood piled up or scattered, stuffed cloth. The air was still heavy with dayheat and smelled, to her fastidious nose, like the old milk and piss of babies, and the trapped human breathing of many days. The few children in evidence were strange and silent, most clung to teachers. And the screens looked battered and primitive, like the ones at the market. There were more teachers than screens.

The teachers who had received her sat down with her on a raised step near the entrance, and stroked her. They told her they were called Var Fadel and Fadar.

"You are not my Fa," said Tasman angrily. She did not know much about adult men, and she did not like the Var, their touch reminded her of medical Book and their body was small, and they were light-voiced and light-skinned.

"We will introduce you to some little friends," said the Var called Fadar, and they took her over to a corner. There, squatting with feet pulled up close against a narrow chest, tow-headed twins about five years old were eating out of a double bowl. Their hair was so strange and light, it was as if a shaft of strong sun covered and blurred them, and Tasman blinked and blinked again. The Fa half-stroked, half-pushed her to persuade her to sit down in front of them, and brought her a bowl with the same food in it—a mess of yeast and banana. Then they left her.

Tasman, finding that no amount of blinking would darken the little boy-heads, began to observe them more closely just as they were. The Twel was eating, and their right hand was "pretending to be Twar," she could see that, and pretending to feed the Twar. But the Twar was not eating. His head looked too small. Not by much, but to glance from one to the other was enough to confirm it. His jaw was small and slack. Though his eyes moved, they did not fix. The right hand pushed food into the slack mouth and it remained there. Tasman's eye caught the Twel's in a reciprocative sharp, scared glance. For once she saw someone who was too absorbed in himself to see or judge her, too much on the defensive to be repulsed or amazed. He went on trying to feed his Twar, not looking at him, pretending the Twar was doing it. Both wore protective muffs on their adjacent ears; Tasman had seen these on babies. When the Twar moved his head, in a clumsy jerk, away from the Twel, their right hand smeared banana on his cheek.

Tasman said, "You are doing that *with both hands*, I saw you."

The Twel stared at her, furious. His own mouth was full of banana, and he had to swallow hastily before he could splutter, "Go away. *Leave-us.*" The formal sounded funny. Tasman backed up a little. He did not look at her again, and pulled their feet in closer. *With both hands* and *with both feet*, thought Tasman. If she said this aloud, what would he do?

It might have been possible to be friends with the tow-headed Twel, who after all had looked at her with clear human dislike, without fear, as an equal and not as a curiosity. Out of eyes so light that they looked as if sand had stuck and clotted the lashes. He was angry with her not because of her malformity but because of her interference. And it was obvious he was going to be loyal to his brother, find in him what comfort and what communication he wanted, or pretend to—it would be a choice encouraged by his parents, and by Book also; the teachers did not try again to intercede for Tasman. She later saw the Twel (the name of these twins was Semer) playing at building a city with the other children, and talking with them, and animatedly bringing his Twar into the game, using their right hand: "Now my Twar is raising the dike—" and the others, though fully aware of the deception, did not deride it.

Tasman liked Semer Twel, in spite of the yellow-white skin and hair, and sometimes, after watching him covertly, she would squat near him and handle the pieces of wood, and try to move her own hands as if one were really hers and the other lifeless, needing her control, but this couldn't interest her. Nor could her liking allow him that silly pretence. Perhaps, in angrily ignoring her, he accepted the fact of her presence, but he did not speak to her again. "Leave-us," that pretentious adult command, was all he ever said, and it was a phrase she could not even have answered back with, as it had no singular.

She explored the screens and found them too simple, and when she asked for pictures for the old tales she was told there none "just here" or "just now." Fadel said, "You may ask for whatever you want, this is Book," but it was a strange Book if the pictures you wanted to learn to read from were not there. What words shall I learn, she wondered, and did not know what else to ask. Finally she recalled the tale of Saduth Twel, and asked for that, but again her teachers denied her. Perhaps tomorrow, they said, indeed ashamed. "We will try to locate it."

"It must be in all Book," insisted Tasman. If they were denying it, they were just too stupid to find it.

Towards morning, more children arrived. There were lively twins on a small raft on wheels, because they could not walk. They were pretty, she thought at first, with a mass of thick, lusterless black hair that was forever entangled. Though they looked only about eight years old, their teeth were already blackened. Tasman wanted to ask them about that, but they stared at her like street children, fascinated and repelled, and then talked softly to each other. Their glances in her direction were deceptive, devious; they were no longer pretty then, and Tasman sensed they'd soon wheel their raft over to the screen and smile with their mouths only, and ask her cruel questions for their own reasons. She ran to Fa and stayed at their feet, lifting her arms to be stroked.

"I don't want those blackteeth to talk to me," she said.

Fadar Var said, "Come, then, and talk to other little friends."

They took her this time across to a low door halfway down the room, leading into a second, smaller room which had no screens, but a lot of sleeping ledges at various heights, and long shallow steps to them covered with rugs. Teachers were sitting with twins there, but stood up and went out when the Fa nodded to them.

Left sitting on the steps was a very small figure. Tasman, led closer, was startled by the great difference on these twins' faces, but then realized that this was because the Twar was bald, or nearly so; he had some tufty baby-hair but his bluish scalp showed clearly. The Twel's hair was cropped short, but thick as fur.

Close up, Tasman knew that the Twar mind was dead. She had heard of this, but it had seemed to her like the tales, and nothing you would encounter in the real world. She stood open-mouthed, staring this time the way she herself was stared at, and the Twel's look, downcast, did not prevent her. Somehow the Twar head had been braced, its very stiffness making it more lifeless. Its eyes, half open, were blue around the lids as if bruised. There was a piece of brown transparent tape or wax on its jawline. There were strange, short marks on its scalp, like drawn lines or cuts healed.

"Twel Kistat, this is Tasman," said the Fa gently, almost in unison. They stooped and stroked his arm and chest but he did not look up. He turned his furry head, still downcast, towards his twin, and began in a slow, dreamy motion to clean the corners of its eyes, and smooth the hairless brows. His hand-hair was twined back around his bony wrist, almost to the elbow, and the dark fingers were small, thin, delicate as a girl's. Tasman knew, with a sudden conviction, that this Twel would not live.

> *Sickness did not kill him,*
> *But he did not wish life.*

The Fa were as good as their word and produced the Saduth tale, and so she learned to read, and demanded the Brother-murder, in which the notorious Twar Yver twisted and heatsealed a garotte on his Twel, out of jealousy, doing it so swiftly that the Twel could not break free: yet the Twel in a final act of almost superhuman strength broke his murderer's neck—revenge even in death was sweet.

"Where did you hear this tale?"

"My mothers are as Tellers. Mamel would have been but for me; they tell many tales to each other; it is an amusement. Sometimes when they think I am asleep."

The Fa compromised, and produced the ballad, as if rhymes made it more acceptable. But it was not really a tale, it was modern, it had happened in this generation.

Because she was ignored or avoided by the other children, Tasman read voraciously. She demanded tales of love and jealousy, the old romances. She only half-wished to read the oldest tales, about the Out-dead, what Mamar had told her was enough for now, and the tales were there, she would read them when she was ready.

She heard no sounds from the second room, and, if she had her way, she would have stayed clear of it. But the Fa took her in every day for a time. Twel Kistat never acknowledged her, and she never heard him speak. The room, the soft thickish steps, seemed to absorb and change and resound the voices of the children and their teachers heard through the doorway, so she could no longer tell what was being said, and heard only a confused clamour. The Kistat, who were very small, seemed smaller and frailer each time she saw them, yet there was a kind of brutish heaviness that seemed to emanate from the dead twin, and the Twel's silence and refusal to look at her, which should have comforted her, made her instead unutterably lonely; and when he moved at all, or began that feeble grooming of the stiff, blue-black head of his twin, she shivered and backed away.

One day, finally, after the Fa and Kistat's teachers had spoken quietly together for a long time, they fetched her to them to persuade her to go in alone;

Tasman stood among them, held gently between the
knees of the Fa, and when she looked into their faces
she could see that they were all watching her directly,
and steadily, and Fadal said, "Just this, Tasman, tell
him it is possible to live." She wanted to refuse, but
they were so unhappy—"beautiful in sadness"—and
she could not; so she walked in stiffly, and stood in
front of the Kistat on the soft floor.

"Twel Kistat, it is possible to live," she said carefully and loudly, as if repeating a letter.

He did not look up. She crouched in front of him,
where he sat on a higher step. She could see up into
his face, and he looked towards her, but whether he
saw her or not she could not tell. She whispered,
"Look at me."

The blind, dead head, fixed on its stalk like a
burnt lamp, was raised while his hung forward. Yet it
was the Twel cheeks that were ruddy, it was he who
was breathing. Suddenly furious, she jumped up and
began to tear at the binding tape behind her shoulders, but she could not find the ties. She burst into
tears. Something gave, and she pulled the sleeve over
her head, and flung Pillowmarie on the floor in a
heap.

"Look at me! It is possible!" she shouted, naked
and stammering, stamping her feet with rage and
futility. Could she have torn that Twar head away as
easily, she'd have done so.

The Twel looked up. His eyes could not cry any
more but he saw her. Perhaps his looks said only, "I
do not want to live like that," or perhaps he had said
this already, once and for all. Her own life, which she
sensed at that moment like a vigorous, crackling fire
in her body, persisted for its own reasons. They could
not understand each other. The Twel turned away,
laying his silent face against his brother's gray temple.

Tasman ran, back to the door where the Fa and the others waited. Then, almost striking against them, she turned and ran back across the rugs again, snatched up her Pillowmarie. They came to meet her. She was embarrassed now and ashamed. "Quick! Put this *on-us!*" Did the Twel Kistat hear her, as she went out with the adults murmuring around her?

5

O ne day she received a visit at Book. These tall, earnest but smiling twins stayed only a short time, but she would have liked them as her teachers, and for a while she believed they would be. They did not approach her, or stroke her or speak to her, but listened and watched from a distance while the Fa talked with her about what she was reading. Did she also draw? Sometimes, she said, she drew while she was listening to Book. Could she show the stranger how she did this?

Tasman drew her version of a Savannah, something like the Saduth pictures, but with many more snakes, made of different coloured lights, while a rather boring Book told her the way numbers advanced and multiplied. It was only a demonstration, neither subject interested her particularly, just then, but turning away from the screen she repeated the numbers, because she wanted to please the stranger.

"And this, say what this is," said Fadel, pointed to Pillowmarie.

"It is not any thing. I used to call it Pillowmarie when I was small. It is so I do not get stared at, so I can live." Anticipating their next question, she added stubbornly, "I wear it either side. I do not correspond to Twel."

Then she was ashamed, because what she was saying was private, the way she talked to her mothers; it did not make sense, and she could tell how the Fa were upset by it, their faces made ugly by her words. But the strange Twel spoke, just once, whether to her or to the Fa she was not sure.

"There are many people, and it is so with me also, who are not Twar mind or Twel mind—it is only an appellation. It is all right to have said this."

The words, in his calm voice, carried great authority, and they comforted her. But the strangers did not touch her, and the Fa said they would not come back again. She was so disappointed that she put them out of her mind. She did not tell her mothers of the visit, and she did not remember it, when she saw them again.

Other events overtook her, the outside world of other people. Though she was unable to make friends at the little Book, and still did not like her teachers, she was learning, and she went at it with a greediness that filled her days. The stares of the blackteethed twins made her miserable, but she was quicker than they could be, and stayed away from them. Had she been able to choose, she would have continued at Book despite the bad parts. But the cars were withdrawn. For a time, Mamel and Mamar found other drivers—big, idle children who were tired of World, but clever in handling machines, who would take the work for a courtesy; they would even drive Travellers out on the long traces to the terminals, beyond which there were no cars, and no directions either, except for the people who—out of joy or curiosity or despair—learned the traceless ways.

The traces of Lofot followed an old road plan. They were part of an older city over which the modern city had built itself in the generations—like Book and the other machines, they now lay deeper than the modern surfaces, the markets and streets and turf roofs and gardens. But because they functioned, they were kept clear and unburied and well–used. What were now the canals had been level streets then, for the sea had since risen; but the traces were diked against the water, they were dusty, dry trenches in which the cars slid away, on old errands that did not always correspond to modern needs.

But the boys began to make excuses, and if they brought Tasman and her mothers to Book they would not take her mothers back again, or bring them to fetch her home in the morning.

"You do not need to *accompany-us*," Tasman offered, but her mothers refused to let her go alone. They remained in that part of the city until the heat of morning. Once, the cars were so late in fetching her from Book, that they almost decided to walk back, but they did not dare walk with her. "We must find a house in this quarter." Then that was what her mothers were doing, all the while she was in Book, looking for a new place to live. No people would have them. Mamel cried when they lay down to sleep.

Then they were stoned. The cars jerked and stopped. It was on the way to Book. "Go on, go on," urged her mothers. Stones banged and pinged on the lid. The cars went on suddenly and fast. At Book, Tas-

man ran in, she did not wait to hear her mothers argu-
ing with the drivers. Her mothers came in again early,
long before daybreak. "We cannot get cars," she
heard them tell the Fa. "We will have to walk, and we
are not sure whether we can protect her."

All the teachers were standing with them inside
the entrance. The Fa were saying, "It is all right. She
can stay here until you arrange something. Medical
Book must agree to that."

What was wrong? If Medical Book agreed to keep
her, would she be returned to the box? Silent, Tasman
waited while they talked and whispered, standing
behind her mothers with her arms lifted under their
heavy arms, her hands held firm and soft in their armpits. Perhaps the Fa liked her mothers, and would let
them stay, too, and sleep with them. She certainly did
not like the Fa, but looking around Mar's arm she
could see that they had placed their hands on her
mothers' breasts, she knew there was sympathy and
she felt a little hopeful.

She ended up staying in Medical Book, some-
where in the large, main building, going to her Book
with the Fa in the evening by an interior path, and seeing her mothers settled in rooms she could not have
reached on her own. She slept with other children on
a long pallet in a room so low that adults had to stoop
to enter it, or move about. There were no boxes, but
the room had that same constant whitish brightness,
the lights did not change colour with the hours, and
this reminded her of the times in the box. The other
children were always drowsy or asleep when she left
them, and when she returned to bed. She supposed
they were sick. Sometimes she cried, missing her
mothers' nearness.

Mamar, Mamel,
Never apart,
Two hands, two breasts,
Two smiles, one heart.

She dreamed in a broken fashion of people bending over her, and once wakened abruptly when a hand, swiftly withdrawn, twitched at her headsleeve, and she stared up at two terrifying, grayish faces, that seemed to twitter and melt before her eyes—scowling looks conjoined with smiles, hideous, like Tellers masking in the market. They went away quickly, climbing hunched over the sleeping children, and she lay awake in fear till the Fa fetched her.

The Fa had arranged it and it was all that could be done. Each day they took her to eat with her mothers. They ate there also. It was a windowless place, probably underground. Mamar and Mamel looked thinner, and tired. After eating, Tasman lay down on the pallet in an adjoining room. She heard low voices.

"Is it possible?" Mamar said, "Are we to be driven out?"

"It is Moonfall hysteria. We can't suggest anything better than to make her a ward of this Book. No one's happy about it, but it has been offered."

That was Fadar speaking; he had a squeaky voice.

She heard Mamel stand up suddenly *with both feet* in her uncouth way; "No" (the emphatic) "That is what the Outdead did to our race, do you realize that? She would be…" Her voice lowered. Someone pulled the curtain down across the opening. Their voices went on for a long time.

6

"Tasman. Tasman, come, we are going away."
She woke up roughly, not sure where she was. She was still in the low alcove beside the rooms her mothers used in Medical Book. And the curtain was pulled up and her mothers stooped in the opening, darkening it. They entered and pulled on her tunic and wrapped the hoods of the sleeves over her head and Pillowmarie. The Fa were behind them, in the larger room, folding up rugs and binding them to their thighs. They went up a ramp and out, all together, half running, a long way by bushy paths across buildings. No one spoke. At a street, they went down into waiting cars. It was short Darkening and the city's lights were a dim orange, very like the dust dusk of twilight, but with a black sky overhead and no moon. The outside air was hot and humid, full of the odour of ixora bushes and firesmoke off the dikes. In the cars, she lay across the laps of her mothers and the Fa. She did not ask where they were going. No stones struck the cars, yet it was as if the adults' bodies were stiffened in anticipation of it, of something bad.

They were not going in the direction of her home, but it seemed to be towards the north, where there was no more city, and when the cars stopped there were no more traces, only a small, disused terminus, slanting into the ground and half-covered with vines.

The Fa helped them up, and they walked a very long way among bushes, while the world's light grew stronger and clearer. Then they passed between a great stand of straight-stemmed forest palms blurred as if with blackish pointed hairs and wrapped with bark like rotten cloth, and the grayish husks of their nuts crumpled underfoot. Tasman thought she could hear water running or breathing, as on a long beach, but no city sounds. The light increased, and between the stems toward the west it seemed more spacious, as if the sea could be there. Finally they came to a low-roofed house at the far side of a yard that had once been cleared but was now a tangle of husks and bushes. It stood half-buried against a wall of forest stems that looked solid, all knit and threaded together with the white branches of softwood trees. In her ear was the certain sound of the sea.

The Fa left them.

Tasman did not return to Book, or to the city in Lofot, for five years. Her mothers told her that Medical Book knew they were there and would provide for them, but not disturb them. No people came to see them except the Fa, and these visits were infrequent.

She was in World now, literally, her days spent at the overgrown tidal stream that skirted the clearing and seeped into the eastern house-wall, and on the great beach that lengthened, the water running out to the horizon and in again, fast and shallow. Great trees grew out of the mouth of the creek and the sand, and laid the red silt far out in a curve, the tiny waves breaking there at odd angles, and the rivulets running after the tide, intricate and changeable. The beach ran,

swiftly becoming water, becoming sand, like a great
breathing. There were no deep, forbidding trenches of
purplish mud, as beyond the city, but it was dangerous to walk far out on the flats and her mothers for-
bade it, though sometimes at Lightening she did so,
late, if they were sleep, when the moon hung pocked
and bloated overhead and really did look closer, as if
she could almost touch it, and the water, almost hot,
warmer even than the air, swilled past her ankles outward, with a hurrying, whispering sound and with
the moon's oil all over it and slithering. To the north-
west, on the horizon, there was a small, low island
that was not always visible; its name was Noss. At
sunset, or when the sun dipped there in late Lightening, it was visible clearly, and few times she had seen
it "turned on its heads"—the main hill and the smaller
one pointed downward and the flat side against the
sky—she would run to tell her mothers—"Noss is
upside down!" and they told her it was a trick of the
light. Sometimes she set out for Noss but it hid; even
bright moonlight would not reveal it, and it would
come no nearer.

Trudging, she would follow the ebb till she
thought she could see, to the south, the glow of the
city past the last point, and till the water was gone
away before her and she stood on bare, hard sand
already crusting dry on the surface, and everything
steady and silent; then she would run back towards
the safe, black-pale fence of the trees, imagining the
water turning and chasing her, a long translucent
wave like a skin or a curtain blowing. The water
returned bearing thin crisp little islets of dried sand
on its skin, the size of her palm or her fingertip, and
she waded by the beach and tried to lift them and they
crumbled.

She came to know every twist of the softwood branches, every shadow and tide-washed root that overhung the sand, every stone in the creek bed. The stream filled, and emptied. Two round pools in the clearing filled and emptied too, twice a day, and they bathed in one of them, it was simple and refreshing; but Mamel said the other one was a pit-pool, for child-birth. Her mothers stayed near the house, except when they climbed after water, because the springs were at a distance inland, and not all clean. Otherwise they harvested salt, told tales, and were idle.

Tasman began to look forward to the Fa's rare visits; when they came she had more freedom than ever, and she got used to them, even to her mother's whispering "Var" on the pallet, but she never liked them. Sometimes she told herself stories like the old romances, and in these stories the Fa were even younger, like big clumsy-spoken boys, and her mothers were not really her mothers, but more beautiful and self-assured. Some predicament had landed them on an island—it seemed to be Noss—and their rescue (which included the dismissal or death by accident of the Fa) was by Travellers arriving on a sea-raft, with beautiful black faces and huge cool hands. Was Tasman there? Not really. But in other stories, she would try to imagine herself loved, the way young girl twins do, crossing hands; but it did not work, her lovers were faceless. Or, remembering the tow-headed Semer Twel and his half-mind twin, she would imagine them well-grown, Twel's look still defiant, and she would tell herself stories that ended, after long, complex trials, with kisses. But she was fastidious: the retarded twin had to be replaced by one who was blind and recovered his sight by some heroic, intuitive deed on her part. Certainly she wanted to court and be courted by the tow-headed Twel first, yet he had to be twinned, as a matter of course, and handsomely. These were stories she created word for word, but never told.

She "looked out of a closed door" in those years, because what she told herself in silence did not correspond to what was, nor was it a tale, bound as it was to her life and how she would change things if she could. Mamar and Mamel did not chide her, though they could see what she was doing, and when she sat with them she knew they saw in her face what she tried to hide from them. They saw her trying to disguise her mind, and what this did to her look—and she could not disguise her mind, teeming as it was with treasonable untold tales that, if they could, would leap out and correspond with what was, reaching to touch her mothers and the Fa with the cool touch of her betrayal.

Once, when they had eaten in the house, and she had turned her head away and was already busy with her thoughts, Mamel spoke to her gently: "Tasman, hear me. You have entered the age when everything comes undone, and if you were with other children, you would see it was the same with them, this secrecy. Don't be ashamed, we were so also, and most girls and many boys, at your age."

She glanced over at them when she heard this, her look still suspicious—for surely no one could have thought what she thought, not to that degree—Mamel went on, however, trying to comfort her: "In one sense, this ugliness is what protects them, for who would desire or force a bond on the half-grown? This is the age before the teeth are blackened when almost all children become devious and soured, they 'enter the minds of snakes' and their faces are disfigured by their minds' voices."

Soon after she was eleven, in Darkening, two events came almost upon one another: her mothers got sick and the Fa took them back to the city. These events were not connected, yet they seemed so, to each other and to her own mind, which despite Mamel's explanations, was not altogether easy. For days her mothers had lain low and feverish in the house. Mamar taught her how to care for their body, which seemed to be leaking, diminishing.

"Are you trying to become pregnant?" she asked them.

"No, we cannot."

"You can, the Fa have been with you. You said it would not happen again, as it did with me—"

"We are sure it would not. But we will not bear any more children. No, this is a sadness in our body, an infection."

"Is it Fa's sadness that has saddened your body?" For she knew that such things, like mind-sadness and other feelings, were contagious.

But they told her no. It was perhaps the old spring water.

By the time the Fa came with their news, her mothers were well enough to receive it happily, though their body had become very thin and weak— they looked old, now, especially Mamel, Tasman thought, seeing them with the eyes of the Fa, who were still young and whose faces were less than beautiful today in their complexity. Perhaps the Fa wanted them closer but not their sickness. Perhaps they would desert them, as her real fathers had done. But she misinterpreted this.

"It is a dispensation and amnesty," said Fadel, after they had embraces and lain down. "We have a letter to say to you, and you can hear this for yourselves. An amnesty for you, and a temporary one for Tasman. Medical Book has arranged it. Do not be worried that Tasman's is temporary. It is a victory."

"But she is too old for your Book now, surely," said Mamar. Tears shone on her cheekbones.

"We do not know what will happen. There are changes in Medical Book. They may want to test her again."

Tasman knelt between them where they lay talking, and placed her hands adult-fashion one on the Fa's chest and one between her mothers' breasts.

"I do not want to go to Medical Book for tests, or live in the city unless I can go to real Book. I will wear a new Pillowmarie if I have to—you will make them again—Mam, but I need to go to Book."

"We do not know what is going to happen to you. We do not believe you have any choice." The Fa Twar placed his hand over hers. "Your mothers need to go home."

7

Whoever had lived in their house had taken good care of it. Much had been renewed. The streets looked smaller, the canal narrower. The dikes had again been raised and the sea was no longer visible from the roof. Tasman realized how happy her mothers were to be back: they touched everything welcome, as she (and they, but less carefully) had touched the leaves and sand and stream and low, fronded doorway in the north farewell. Here, though larger and very clean, the two rooms seemed hollow and dull. Parts had been raised into platforms against the damp, and the floor was slick and hard, almost shiny with use. Tasman, crouching to look at the wall under a shelf, where she had once hidden a small white stone, saw that it had been revealed and polished, and that four other stones were set around it, and because of this she thought that there had been children here, although she found no other evidence.

The lights of the city she had stared after from the north seemed less magical than she remembered them, and far less radiant than the stars she had watched on moonless nights from the beach. Worse, it was not possible to go about freely. She wore a new Pillowmarie (that she herself helped to fashion, breaking off dried grass from the roof), but wherever she walked the looks she got shrivelled her courage. And her mothers did not encourage her, they were uneasy unless she was home. It was best to be indoors or on the roof, where she had made a kind of bower, and she put Pillowmarie aside again. The Fa came often and stayed with her mothers sometimes but they looked restless; it seemed as if they came with rumours rather than news. "There is no letter, there is no news," she was told, and this was to reassure her, she felt. It was obviously out of the question to expect to go to Book, and she no longer asked, but she thought of it stubbornly. And she became apprehensive whenever she saw them: would they have a letter this time, would she be forced to go into Medical Book, and be tested? What did that mean? Past the roof, the city shone and changed colour and sounded. Tasman waited.

One day she came in off the roof when the Fa had been and gone and had not called her. Her mothers lay on the pallet. Mamar was caressing Mamel's face, which was streaked with tired tears. Mamel's eyes were closed.

"Is she asleep?" asked Tasman, but it was Mamel who answered, "Almost," and the hand gently pushed itself away. Mamar lay back, and gestured for Tasman to sit down. She turned her face from Mamel.

"It has been worked out. You are to go away, to live in a city called Uppsal, and do Book there," she said in a forced, level voice.

Tasman stared. "Is this decided?"

"Yes" (the emphatic).

Mamar went on: "It is in the Savannas. Good men have told us in a letter brought by a Traveller, that you can live there. It is a great Book, and a very old one."

"It is their Book, then, and will not be mine," said Tasman, and burst into tears.

"Tasman. It's true it will be their Book, but it is not medical, the Fa have also assured us of this. And Medical Book here is not happy that you are going but they have been overruled. It is a place where you can learn much and be protected. Do you understand this?"

Tasman was silent.

"If you stay here, you cannot remain with us and you cannot perhaps live. This is how it is for you."

"I would wish to be treated as an adult, even if my teeth are white as milk. I would wish to hear the letters."

"We have not yet learned them. The Fa will tell you them, surely, when they return, word for word. We will have a good leavetaking. We will finish with it, I promise you."

They sat up suddenly and Mamel, jerked awake, stared at Tasman with wide, frightened eyes that suddenly swam with tears. "It is not finished but it will be finished," said Mamar, as much to her Twel as to Tasman. They pulled her in against their breasts. She shut her eyes against their heart but she could still see the incompleteness in Mamel's face.

"The old will be finished before the new is allowed to begin," quoted Mamar, her voice breaking. "Good men will come for you."

"It will be within the year, quite soon," she went on more calmly. "Before it is too hot to travel."

8

They came at first Lightening, the Sorud, standing very tall across the doorway, and she thought this was how her fathers must have looked—so distant and courteous and upright, with their blackened teeth and large, widely-spaced eyes. Their hair was long and thick and loosely twined, hanging between their heads and dividing their chest with a single braid whose endstrands were bleached almost white, as she heard the hair of Savannah-people can be. Sorud Twar had a much broader face, the jaw-muscles and mouth-muscles were very thick and mobile, and it was he who spoke and laughed and smiled. Sorud Twel was silent, his face rather gaunt and inward, yet with no deviation, and she felt him inviting her to come to them, and when they were seated she sat on the floor close to his hand. But it did not move, only the Twar's caresses of courtesy acknowledged her as he spoke to her mothers, and touched her almost absentmindedly in the way of adults touching children, light strokes, up and down her back and sides and arms.

The private leavetaking and the formal one were both over. Tasman had no more crying left to do, nor did her mothers; they saw each other expressionlessly, grief had wrung them well. And she had said goodbye to the Fa also, forgiving them in tears if rage; no longer jealous, she could see clearly their lovebond to her mothers as she put it behind her. Now she was no longer there to hinder it, they would be housebonded surely, and the thought passed her without weight or importance. And she touched the house intimately in all its particulars, just as she had touched their faces, so that now as she crossed the rooms for the last time she sensed them as dreamy and withdrawn. She was ready.

The trip south to the terminus took most of the day. She lay against the Sorud in the heat of the cars in a kind of exhaustion of spirit, but did not sleep. The Twar again caressed her, his hand moving slowly the length of her gloved foot, touching the arch and ankle, then moving slowly up her legs and sides and arms.

Then she felt the Twel hand move very gently to her shoulder and across her throat to the meeting of her clavicles, the "salt cellars" there which were in her case so pinched and strange, his narrow adult fingers very gently pressing there and touching. "Are you of

Medical Book?" she asked, but she was not afraid, because there was difference in his touch.

"No," he said, using the emphatic, that broached no argument. "Historical, it is called." She had never heard that word.

"It was I who named you, Tasman," he said. "I sent that name in a letter eleven years ago, in answer to a request from the Namers of your city. I saw you once again, when you were six. I have never forgotten you."

Later he was to tell her, "I believe you are truly one of the Outdead. And I do not believe they were terrible savages, even though they did their best to destroy us, and nearly succeeded. They were also people, their race walked, and you will learn this. We have archives that tell good tales about them, they lived and did Book under this very place where we live. When we become less afraid of our past, we will be able to remember these things. And sometimes, Tasman, when I have had my head inside their Book for many nights, and thought only of these things, and I look up and see you, I see who you really are."

He did not say these things now, but they were contained in the strange word he had used, and in his touch, which was curious but not like the Medical Book which had touched her there and measured her and made her fell even more deformed with their prods and stares.

Twel's fingers moved around her naked neck, her throat so small in the far-too-loose single sleeve the Mar had sewn her, frail and exposed like a stem without leaves, a stripped branch. They slid behind her ears, and reaching down seemed to draw and gather her narrow shoulders upward, joining her sad, simple head to her body by their large and quiet stroke—a completion and together-sensing. Her nape tingled, and the surface muscles of her face; she felt them changing at the edges of her eyes, like another layer or cloth of sadness acknowledged, discarded, that she had not known she was wearing always. He is making me beautiful, she thought; his touch was different than anyone else's had ever been, even her mothers'.

They reached the end of the traces. The terminus at Uppsal lay far away in the northern Savannas, and from here they would walk. The Sorud stretched, and lifted her up out of the cars, and then took out their provisions, strapping them across their upper arms and thighs. They rebound their foothair around their ankles, for it was late and the sand would soon be cool, and Tasman, seeing them do this, pulled off her cumbersome footgloves, and she felt on her bald feet the heat of the world. She stared about her.

There was not even scrub forest now, only low bushes that even in the amber dust-laden sunlight of afternoon looked gray, as if spilled over with ashes. They began to walk southeastward between these bushes, the sand underfoot paler and less red than the clay in Lofot, and in some places freshly blown across the path. Their shadows flowed and lengthened before them, the Sorud shadow normal and comfortable, spreading large to its shoulders' breadth and their heads almost exactly outlining the path's direction, as if they were telling the way, and hers leaping along twarside, tiny and skinny, as if it were made by a cloth or staff. She stopped seeing it, and raised her eyes to the hills whose long lines imperceptibly swung and changed as they walked, and the broad sky still simmering with heat, almost pink overhead, and near the hills ruddy in the sundust. Close by, a great ashy bush, or a depression, or a cluster of spiked grass, forced her to look down, and she saw and saw again the place where her fathers had fallen. The dry earth reached between her toes, and smelled sweet, some herb she seemed to recall but could not name. The rosy shadows between the hills swelled out of the hollows as the sun dipped behind them to the north-west.

Sorud Twel was silent, but as it cooled the Twar began to talk, and told her about Uppsal, and where she would live, just as he had told her mothers but now more simply—with them, eating out of their bowl and drinking from their cloth. He told her too about their Book, but she could not imagine it; it was very deep, he said, and cool, there were real things in it, as well as screens and copies, it was like the tales of the ruins, but it was not a ruin, it was a modern city.

She did not ask, but she did not think there were children at the Uppsal Book, certainly not where she would be with the Sorud—and she was determined she would keep close to them—and this was good, because she had never felt like children, and did not now. She walked taller at the Sorud's side.

The Twar told her also about the Savannas, and Tasman guessed that it was he who loved to go roving there, away from the city; it was because of him that they were Travellers, and that their hair was bleached white.

"There is a great plain to the east, and they say it is an old sea bed, at least, Twel says so, and he is called a Great Authority." Twar laughed softly. "There are many wells there, and yeast farms, it is not all wild. But farther east it is wild, and at Kaamos we have gone farther, making fires and paths, it is not so dark even at late Darkening, we can see even on moonless nights by the stars, and it is cooler then. Twel sleeps, but there is a ruin we will go to soon, and he dreams of that place, because it was a great city in the time of the Outdead, and it is accessible, we have been told. It is farther than the ruin Lenh."

"I have never been to World with other children," said Tasman, "but I have played on the shore, also in Darkening, all the time we lived north of the city."

"Then you will go to World with me." His voice was full and joyous.

She walked until nightfall, holding the Twar's large hand and listening to him, and then they lifted her up and carried her, baby-fashion, her legs strad-dling their hip-bundles on either side, and what she guessed was not the bundles but their own, darker burden, alive and comfortable between her thighs as they strode forward. She remembered part of an old song: *When our teeth are mad black / when we are touched in the new-old places.* Her bare feet hung free.

Weary, she pressed her face into their braided hair, that smelled stale and good, like woodsmoke. The air was cooling. The Twar's hand caressed her back and shoulder blades, up and down, but she kept herself awake, until at last it stayed, supporting her; and then she felt the Twel hand, harmonious, release its support and move to her vestigial seventh cervical, and cover her nape and rest there. Then, she allowed herself to fall asleep.

two

9

Uppsal to Lofot at Esmenvar in the street of jasmines, 441 Lightening, the fourth month, to my mothers.

My mothers, I am telling this letter to Travellers who are preparing to go to Lofot. I am well. I have heard nothing from you. No one has made that journey since I came here with the Sorud five months ago. I will soon be twelve years old, but I am not yet an adult woman.

I will tell you how I live in this city. Twel Sorud is, I believe, important here, and when people come to see him they are very courteous and wait for him to speak. We live in the west part which is indeed a great Book, but the oldest part is underground. There is no forest of any kind, and no sea. I have been across the city with the Sorud at night, and east of it there are habitable plains and great farms. That part of the city is something like Lofot because of the lights, but there are no canals or flowering trees. Twel Sorud has told me there are great wells under the city. Where we live is quite cool and pleasant. I do not see many other people. I live in the Sorud's apartments, which are large, and built around a tower made of rough stones, and they open down into Book. Twel Sorud reads Book there every day. He is teaching me many things, and I am learning what it is about, to be a Historian. Most of the day, I watch what he is doing.

Twar Sorud is, however, urgent to travel, and as soon as it is cooler, we are going to journey to Lenh, and perhaps to a ruin farther than Lenh, where no one has been. But it is inside the Sheath of the world, and many people say it will be impossible. The Sorud have been to Lenh, because Twel studied there for some years, and they lived there. But it is a ruin, and no one goes or stays there except people who are studying Book. At night, Twar likes best to go outside the city and walk in the desert. One thing I can tell you about the desert, there are not many snakes there after all and I have never seen one, but the Twar has.

I cannot go about freely here, but with the Sorud no one can harm me. I eat from their bowl and sleep on their pallet, as it was agreed. They are kind to me. When I become an adult, the women who will *attend-us* are the Say.

They come to these apartments and I talk with them sometimes, but they are not bonded to the Sorud.

Twel Sorud asks me to tell you that he is pleased with me, and that my mind is so retentive, that I could be a Teller myself. I am learning many new tales. This Book is different, because it contains some remnants that Twel calls "true book", but I have not seen these things, though they are what Twel is concerned with. There are some other, quite young twins who study sometimes with Twel, but he says I am quicker. The Twel continues very serious, but Twar Sorud plays with me sometimes. The only thing is, that if they go away at night, because Twar is restless, then I am often left behind. Twar is preparing very carefully for our journey.

Greet the Fa. I remember you in quietness. *Remain as you were when we took leave of you, so that our minds, and your minds, are in harmony with the world.* The Sorud greet you.

Tasman.

When Tasman tired of Book she could go in to the tower. Though it was underground and surrounded by other, newer walls, she could pretend that it still looked out on ancient Uppsal-a. Twar Sorud pretends this too, she thought, and he would not be ashamed to imagine the scenes below these windows, the streets where the race they called the Outdead walked to and fro in ancient days.

Sorud Twel was not just concerned with "true book," as Tasman had said in her letter. He was, she discovered, involved in an occupation she had never considered—he wrote Book, he knew how to write.

"Why are you so surprised at this? Did it never occur to you that someone must write things down?" He gave her a rare smile.

They were sitting in the outer room, a small area behind the tower, which was next to the apartments and which belonged as much to Twel as to the huge Book that extended beyond and below it. His screen glowed before them. It seemed natural that words should be summoned out of Book and appear here to be read, but today, when Tasman joined the Sorud, Twel's hand was creating them—words in a new order, coming new from the quick motion of his hand.

She leaned up against their body, and Twar embraced her and pulled her half onto their lap.

"Will you teach her to write?" he asked his Twel softly, his voice a little teasing.

Tasman stiffened. "It is forbidden," she whispered.

"I will not teach you then, Tasman, not as long as you are afraid, but I have no way of stopping you from learning. I do write Book, and you are too quick not to learn, if you continue to watch and mimic me the way you do."

"Will you apply for me," she stammered, "so I may learn this?"

"Then he would have to apply to himself," laughed Twar, stroking her. "You are safe with him, little Tasman, learn what you like."

Twel went on writing on his screen, and Tasman, not understanding how his hand assembled his thoughts, turned to the screen on its right. It was really Twar's but he never used it. She drew, randomly. She could draw, and from this skill she thought that she could form something like words. Frightened but a little reassured, she let the lines move, so that the lines she drew with lights became great, wobbly letters, and she framed her first word, and read it: SMAN, and then beginning again, TAS-MAN, and then, *WE-ARE* TASMAN. Her scalp tingled with excitement. A new play had begun.

Within a short time she was able, in this way, which was like drawing, to write whatever she liked. It was a case of remembering in her mind the way a word would read, and copying that image, and soon it became simple. But the Twar, using the panel, could make words appear as in Book, and when she asked him whether what he wrote went into Book, and became Book, he answered Yes, he had only to enter it, and it was available to all Book.

"Anywhere in the world? Even in Lofot?"

"Yes."

"Even in Manj'u?"

"I do not know. Manj'u is a great distance away, Tasman." She noticed a change in his voice, a wariness.

"So is Lofot, and Whalsey, and—"

"Not so far."

"My mothers told me it is a great Book about Moonfall, about how to prevent Moonfall. Do you not read this? Is that not entered?"

Twel was silent for a time, his face closed. Finally he said, "It is not entered. And whether Manj'u is a Book, or a city of religious hysterics, I am not sure. Do not worry about Moonfall. There is no danger to us."

"Are you not afraid?" Tasman remembered what she had been told, the predictions of the Lofot street-tellers, the threats and promises.

"It is so distant in the future that it cannot concern us."

"But Twel, why is it that there is nothing written about Moonfall in Book?"

She saw his face change then, and read his anger in the downward scowl of his steep cheek, the gaunt hollows in front of his clenched jaw-muscles, the thrust of the depressors under his lip. "It has not happened, therefore nothing can be written about it. I know you have heard tales and songs in Lofot market, or from your mothers. It is speculation."

He drew her in under his arm, his face softening. "Tasman, where there is fear, and hope, and speculation, there can be no harmony. And what is to happen corresponds to nothing. It cannot. It does not exist."

"But in Manj'u—"

"We do not know what is happening in Manj'u. No Travellers have come from there in this generation to tell us. These are songs and tales, Tasman."

"The students Gershon said that it is you who have prevented Moonfall tales from being in Book."

He looked past her, his face resuming the closed, knotted look that, if she had not known him, would have terrified her.

"Yes. I have prevented it, and I will continue to prevent it."

"—They have been no friends to you either, Tasman," he went on presently. "These Moonfall fools."

"I know." She leaned on his shoulder. "Twel Sorud, everyone talks about Moonfall in Lofot, and everyone is not a fool."

The Twar burst out laughing. "Everyone is a fool more or less, except my brother. Tasman, don't be distressed. It is not just in Lofot that Moonfall is preached and sung. But in this house and in this Book, it is not a popular subject."

"What is true," said Twel evenly, "is what has happened. I am a man who is interested in that only."

"My brother was born with an enormous curiosity, and his head has corridors for amassing fact, without end," said Twar half-seriously. "He would like to persuade us that recovering the past is more useful than inventing the future. He is not always success-ful."

Twel hugged Tasman, and gently pushed her off their lap so she stood before them.

"I am successful, if I prevent Moonfall from being written into Book. And I have students. The past is being returned to us. This Book thrives."

"I am going to be your student," said Tasman stoutly.

"You are my student already! My best student, and my bridge. Whatever is happening, has hap-pened."

Tasman, embarrassed by his praise and unsure what he meant, turned away.

In bed, she whispered and laughed with the Twar, and dared to tell him some of the tales she had invented when she lived in hiding with her mothers, north of Lofot.

"That tale is good," he whispered one night, stroking her face with his large hand, pushing back the low-growing hair on her forehead. "Why do you not write it?"

"Write it—no, I could not." Shyly—"It would take a long time."

"Twel could enter it in Book, and other children could read it, twins here, who have never seen the sea, or islands, or the return of the tide."

"But I would be ashamed."

"There is no need. Who has written the tales in Book? Do you think those people are more intelligent or seemly than you?"

"But those are told-tales."

"Not all. You know that some are modern."

"Twel, Tasman has a tale for Book. I suggested that she write it. I think it would please her."

The twins lay face to face. It was early, and the low sun of Lightening already sought out the seams in the lofty ceiling and made reams and strands along the curtains. She slept, twarside, curled under his out-flung arm.

"It would take her a long time, and I do not know whether she would let me transcribe it for her from those letter-lines she draws. She is still very frightened."

"Could she not tell it you, as do the Tellers? She was brought up on tales, her mothers were very romantic. Their heads were full of stories."

"She has heard a great deal she need not have heard."

"Ah—they lived very proscribed lives because of her. It was their only amusement. They are very intelligent—the Twel was a Teller, or ready to be one, I believe."

But Tasman, stubborn, refused to "tell the tale into Book" as Twar suggested. But in the tower, she blew on the tiny restored panes of the windows, and drew words with her finger, and slowly formed it. And, beside Twel, she began to watch what he wrote, the complex panel, the swiftly moving hand. And eventually, with many errors, she printed it, and repaired it, while Twar, smiling, watched, and Twel went on working, pretending not to be aware.

The Tale of the Island

The Ismay lived on an island under the moon. When the tide ebbed, the sand stretched as far as the eye could see. When the tide flowed, the water ran right up under the trees, which were so thick stemmed they could not be walked between. At ebb tide, the Ismay walked a little way around the island, and then ran back. They lived in the open, because the rain was warm, and the tree fronds sheltered them from the sun at Lightening. Every day Ismay Twel cleared back the vegetation and then sat and looked out over the sea.

Her sister was asleep. She breathed softly but did not eat. Twel did everything by herself. She wished her sister would awaken, but she did not know how to awaken her. Once, when they had first come to the island, that twin had eaten a poisonous fruit. Though she had only put it into her mouth and then spat it out, the poison had entered her brain through the roof of her mouth, and she had been asleep ever since.

Her head hung forward and her long hair hung down. Ismay Twel was afraid to try to go all the way around the island. She could not remember that they could swim, because she had never been told of this. She was afraid of the sea.

On the far side of the island, the west side, lived twins whose name was Semer. They had arrived on a raft. But the Twar was blind, because he had been hurt, and had lain without consciousness on the raft, staring into the sun, for some days.

The Semer also had a clearing against the beach. But they were not afraid of the sea.

Their raft was gone, but one day a tree fell into the water. We will begin and end at this tree, said Twel. We will walk at ebb tide along the shore. They walked farther at each ebb, and at

sea-return they held on to the stems and
branches at the bank, half-swimming, and
after some days they came around to the other
side of the island and saw the Ismay sitting
beside the beach.

Ismay Twel was very afraid to see them.

What Semer Twel saw was, beautiful twin girls
eleven years old, and the Twar asleep. What
Ismay Twel saw was, beautiful twin boys
eleven years old, and the Twar blind. The
Semer had rope-coloured hair that hung to
their waists, but the Ismay were swart, as it is
in this country.

The Semer encouraged Ismay Twel to swim,
and when the seawater entered the sleeping
Twar's mouth, she began to choke and to
breathe very hard and cough, and she began to
wake up. But blind Semer did not improve,
and Ismay Twel felt pity for him. So she sealed
his eyes shut with spit and aboro leaves, so
they received more and more darkness, and
after twenty days she removed the leaves, and
he reopened his eyes, and could see a little.
When they lay in the clearing, *Beginning-to-
waken* looked into Semer Twel's eyes, and
Beginning-to-see looked into Ismay Twel's eyes,
and they loved each other. Then they were
healed and happy, and kissed, and lived well
on the island. They named the island Kr,
because they did not know its name.

"You may enter it," said Twel Sorud when the
story was perfected. She touched the lights he showed
her, and laughed, turning in against their body, and
hugged them with shyness and delight.

"It is only a silly children's tale," she said.

"It is better than much in Book," said Twar. "You have no idea how much trash there is in Book, Tasman. That is why I never read."

"You cannot, that is why you do not," she laughed, pulling his ear.

She looked up into their faces. His was teasing and tender, the broad muscles of his mouth trying not to smile. Twel's was gentle as almost always, more gaunt and abstracted. He said nothing, but she knew he was proud of her. Her heart swelled.

"It was not so very dangerous, after all," she said.

"You are pleased with her story," said Twar to his brother, that night as she slept.

"Yes. We must encourage her. This is perhaps the beginning of writing about herself."

"You will not say this to her—it is not necessary, Twel."

"No, she believes she is playing. But she is approaching it. She can make a valuable story of it, when she dares."

10

One day while Tasman was in the tower, she saw the first seeping of her blood, and knew she had reached adulthood.

The Say came, and she went with them into the room that would now be hers. She had not seen it before, though she knew it was prepared. It was on the surface, on a hill, so that the narrower part, facing northeast, was on a slightly lower level. There was no exit, but a long open strip of sky showed under the roof. The room was chalked white, and there was a thin, fine rug on the pallet, and on the floor, a rug made of human hair: this rug was very, very old but very strong. She had seen such rugs in the other apartments, but not this one or this patterning. There was red hair in it, in a design of small broken circles like the waxed moon. It was gift from the Sorud. Her room opened from their apartments, above a short stair.

Tasman was shy of the Say. They were what is called "true twins," their minds so similar it was difficult, really impossible, to think of them as separate beings at all. The identical faces held identical expressions; if one was sad it was as if the other, intuitively, became sad also. True twins did not converse, having no need. Such symbiosis was rare, though degrees of it were not uncommon, but twins born like the Say had almost to be forced to learn speech, though they walked early (this was a sign of them)—sometimes as early as three years. The women were as good as barred from having children, because it was said that their children never prospered. So they are root all their lives.

The Say received her. Female twins' initiation into womanhood was simple but took time—all the days of their first menses. The only remarkable change in Tasman, when she emerged, would be her blackened teeth—the sign of adulthood. And on the last day she would eat root, enough for nine years.

The Say had black, massy hair and dark ruddy cheeks. Though their eyes were broadly set, they had, when they were with Tasman, the diffident, closed manner she had grown to expect from strangers. The Sorud tried to encourage them to relax with her, and be kind to her, she knew—because when they were all together Sorud Twel would speak often to her, and Sorud Twar would almost exaggerate his own easy behaviour with her, keeping her close to him, stroking her. But it had not helped. No, she thought as she entered the new room, only Twar likes me, and only Twel takes me seriously, it is only with them I feel at home, and comfortable. And she missed them, closed in the upper room with the Say. The days seemed interminable.

"Smile now, speak now, look at your adult faces." She saw in the silvered glass they held for her the result of the blackening, and was satisfied, though the wide pane gaped, where only one face looked back. Then mouthsore she fasted, and on the day the blood ceased, ate root and returned to the Sorud.

On the second night after Tasman returned as an adult, the Sorud lay mouth to mouth, conversing softly, though they were alone.

"I am sure she dislikes sleeping in her room unable to speak to anyone," said Twar.

Twel drew a deep breath. "I miss her here also. Think of her. We are not even as her fathers. If she wants to he short-bonded to us—"

Their body's response was immediate and unequivocal, so that Twel experienced a rush of relief. He had not been sure of his Twar, his twin to whom he allowed the pleasure of strength he himself was less interested in, or took for granted. He had hoped

Twar would wish this, but he had not been certain. They had lived in the same body all their lives, and Twar's tastes still surprised him, they had shared adventures that had taken him completely by surprise—and, who would have been able to predict, from Twar's easy behaviour with Tasman, that this vague, adult attention would or should alter? It was not natural that the short-bond should be between those who had been previously on such intimate terms.

"But then," he said aloud, "nothing about Tasman can be natural, we cannot expect that."

Twar, understanding him, assented. "I am well used to her, though I never shared your obsession with the Outdead. She is about so much that I am not particularly aware of what she looks like any more." He paused. "And also, I don't find that—unattractive." Again, their body responded, urgently. "Are you going to approach her?" he asked.

"Why do you defer to me?" asked Twel a little angrily. "No, let us see how this goes on. Let us allow her some time." He turned his face away.

"I will have to touch her surely," said Twar in his low voice, speaking into Twel's ear. "She is an adult, if I do not touch her she will reason that it is because of her birthfault, and she'll get that ugly, defiant look —what she has with the Say, and strangers. Poor little mind."

"I do not know. She knows she is safe with us. I think she will come to us. She is not so much an adult that she can be feeling comfortable—I think, she cannot be happy in there all by herself, the little one."

They lay for a long time, both wide awake now, in the surprise of their decision and their desire.

It was lonely in her room. Tasman turned and turned on the pallet. To be an adult, was this to mean never to climb about on the Sorud any more, play with their handhair, pleating it outlandishly across their hands and teasing them? Worse, never again to lie curled twarside all night, easy and unscared? It would not be seemly to go to them now. But what was changed? She ran her tongue over her teeth, so smooth they felt now, and slippery. She was an adult. "Touch us where we have not been touched," said the song. But she was afraid. She was too proud to ask to be short-bonded. Not everyone was, it was not the inevitable outcome of initiation, this would be their excuse. No one else could accept her as they did, and if any could, she did not believe the Sorud would let her go. She remembered coming out of the new room and running down the stair to show them her adult smile. But they were not in the apartments, and when they returned, the Say were with her. Everything was polite, the first urge to rush at them, embrace them, was past, an awful shyness go hold of her and before the Say left she went back to her room. Her mouth tasted of root and she could not think of food, though she had fasted four days.

And she stayed there, and they did not come to her or summon her. And she slept, restlessly, and today, though she went to the screens and sat by them, and watched Twel working, the Twar did not draw her to them as was his way, and she held herself stiffly apart from them. They went up on the roof for the moon's wind at twilight, and they talked about unimportant things. When they sat down to eat, they courteously gave her a new bowl, so that she could not even reach into their bowls any more, leaning close against them.

She went into the tower, leaving them at the table, and wished them to come to her, but her wish did not correspond, they had not come and she cried, the food out of the lonely bowl and the root taste and her slippery teeth combined with the sound of her own voice softly crying; if this was the rest of her life, the awful taste of adulthood, what was to become of her?

She was like the tower that was no longer a tower in the open air, but closed in by other levels and walls. She did not dare go back to them, but went quietly to her own room.

Eventually toward morning she slept, dully, for a few hours, and woke with her hair wet with sweat. Before thought, she jumped up to go to them, her body's natural turning towards the only comfort she knew. And met them at the foot of the stairs.

Twar lifted her "with both hands," and carried her against their body, warm, welcoming, back to their own bed.

11

They were tender, and very slow. It was days before they presumed to ask anything of her, they insisted on her passivity. No one came near them. If the screens and scholars complained, they did not know of it; if any came for Twel Sorud's counsel or knowledge, it was necessary to go away again with nothing.

Their intent was all inward, all concentrated here, and contained.

Tasman lay in a drowse, allowing them anything, out of shame not letting herself speak or cry out or sigh. Twar's hand, the great hand that had held and stroked her so often before, moved even more carefully now as it crossed her breast under the sweat-soaked shift, the thumb and fingers sucking the nipple forward. His mouth received it through the wet cloth. Then she felt Twel's mouth, closing on her other breast. They shifted their body a little, as it lay over her, half propped on their arms to ease their weight. Twar released her and pulled at the shift with his teeth, nuzzled it higher so her left breast slipped free. Again his hand shaped it forward, his wide lips closed over nipple and black areola: she looked down, saw his foreshortened face, his broad jaw, the cheek-muscles pulling. Then through the cloth, Twel's tongue flicked hard across her other nipple, and she looked at him, and saw that he was watching her face intently, flicking, flicking and watching. She wanted to hide from those eyes, her face felt so naked, and she turned her head away, and saw the threads of light, the dust motes overhead. Daylight far up at the rafter slits, earth walls of rubbed clay, the tower wall swelling inward on one side, its rough stone. Long, brown rugs hung down the outer wall, shadowy in their folds. The rugs under her were twisted and dragged sideways, or perhaps she lay sideways, the room wavering. Between her legs, wetness slid that was more than sweat. Their penis lay swollen against her inner calves, her legs tightened on it, what was there was alive, and answered the pressure, it felt as if it was as large as her own legs, she was afraid of it. She looked back at them, her mouth parting. Someone was making a sound, it was her own voice, coming out of her mouth. The Twel watched her still, his look unreadable, and she let her eyes lock into his, though she knew how naked her look was, how scared and ardent and ashamed.

They bathed her, allowing her to do nothing. Cool wet cloths stroked her, her limp arms were lifted and they wiped her armpits, the cloth was drawn across her eyes and temples and mouth. They gave her water and salt to drink. Then her body was lifted, turned, slowly washed with coolness, their eyes watching her body as they moved her; they squeezed out the cloths again, drew them across round surfaces, through creases and folds. Twel Sorud watching her face. The Twar parted her downy thighs, washed her intimately. His hand, his two fingers inside the thin cloth, moving slowly downward, downward and then a little inward. The Twel arm lifting her a little, his cheek and mouth leaning against her thigh, watching, and then watching her face. Again, downward and then a little inward. Her gaze again locked in the Twel's, she could not remember whose fingers, unclothed, began to circle the small place where the mound parted, rather quickly and quicker, as the slow cloth went on stroking, and gently pressed. There was a kind of beat to it, the way the heart's thud is echoed in the markets by the Tellers' wrist against the earth, when they begin, and then quicken it, a closing in of the fingers on a certain centre into which her body wanted to pour itself, as through something narrow and fiery and difficult, she sensed herself arching higher than the Twel had raised her, and saw his mouth part as he stared at her face, his brow contracted in a frown she could not read or attend to. She felt her secrecy, in its severest hiding-place, her very self burst through those fingers, spill out, melt down. And his eyes, shining, never leaving her face. The cloth pressed, deep and wet, and the Twar hand covered her where she shuddered, and she slid back into the Twel arm as it released her. They lay down, drawing her half in under their breast, their dishevelled hair was dragged across her face and she could hear their heart pounding against her temple.

"We want to enter you now," said Twar, over her head, his voice very low and blurred and heavy. "Will you let us enter you."

But they did not, not for hours, days. She became more used to them, to their nakedness, so that sometimes, when she herself was released and swimming in a half-sleep, it seemed not so much scary as funny, and she wanted to tease them for their want. But their caresses turned her serious again, and what lay along her body was not funny but intriguing and alien, she was curious but they would not let her touch them there, they kept her passive, though she felt its heaviness pull along her side when they moved, or flop and find a place between her legs or buttocks.

They played with her. What Twar had said, in his extremity, was said more rarely now and she knew they did not want an answer. Loosely sitting, she bent over them as they lay with their heads in her lap, Twel's mouth on her breast, his teeth clinging at the base of her nipple, and Twar's tongue between her thighs, almost sharp, pointing in, the beat of their tongues beginning as they listened for the beat of her breath, increasing speed as she did, till she flung herself back, rolled over and away from them in shame and joy. Then the blunt nudge, pushing between her buttocks, the soft noise of flesh on flesh. "We want to enter you now." Twar's voice, heavy over her head.

It was in her room, where they had carried her squirming and unfinished, after what seemed to her hours of a series of sequences that they broke off just before the end. Twel had watched her face, and they had drawn back each time, and drawn back her own hands, so she was half-fighting with them. She resisted, and a new, wild, scared delight opened its eye for one instant, but they pinioned her wrists, licked, pushed, withdrew. As they carried her now she was half-crying, shivering. In her room, they sat down and she slid down their body, their penis upright between her belly and theirs; they moved and then it was behind her, then, as they lifted her, found where it would be—easily. She felt proud, swollen, frightened, and suddenly cold. Her eyes sought the Twel's and saw a hard look, grayish, as if his face had turned to stone. The Twar's eyes, when she turned to him, were shut, as if in effort. Their faces terrified her, so distant and perfected. They shifted a little and lay back, keeping her against them. Then they rolled carefully over, but she was a moment too slow, and they slid apart. Twar gasped, said something. She felt the human hair rug under her back, dry and cold. There was a kind of silence in the place. She tried to speak, clearing her throat. "Take me back." They stood up, releasing her. Following them down the stair, she staggered, and realized she had not walked, or eaten, or even been out of their touch for days.

Their pallet was still warm and the room smelled rank and thick. The rugs were hugely messed, as after a stormflood, most of them on the floor. The Sorud sat down on the pallet, and she dropped into their arms. They rocked her, and rocked her.

When their lives resumed some sort of order, and they worked and planned and walked again, and the

Sorud made love to Tasman but also ate and slept, things did not seem so different, and being an adult was not so strange after all. She was seldom in her own room, and one day she folded the human hair rug and took it to the tower. She slept on the Sorud's pallet.

It was day. The Sorud spoke into each other's mouths. "She remarked," said Twar half-amused, "that perhaps in Uppsal the short-bonded never kiss? You heard that? Are you aware that we have never kissed her?"

Twel lifted his head, looking across his brother's profile at Tasman's sleeping face. It was still strange to him, how she lay on her side. There was a picture in true book, someone in red lying on his side—Breughel—he would find it, compare her ways—

Her postures ought to be drawn, he supposed, for Book. But "She was probably drawn like that for Medical Book when her body was infant," he said aloud, finishing his thought.

"Twel, speak to me."

"It is something we cannot well talk about," said Twel, lying back.

"Ah—if she is unhappy about it—"

"She has a fierce sense of justice."

"It is those old tales her mothers filled her with," said Twar. He sighed, and stretched their body luxuriously. "The romances, the jealousies." He turned to his brother again, suddenly serious. "As you already know, I did not answer her."

"She is still passive. She will kiss us when she decides to."

"She is not so passive. She is learning how to delight us. But she does not know what to do about

73

this. She still lies Twarside out of habit. But she looks to you. I have seen it."

Twel felt the warm breath from his brother's mouth and was aware that his own throat was constricted, he had been holding his breath. He loosed it deliberately.

"You want to kiss her."

"I want what she wants. It is no small thing. We are bonded. Yes, I would like it, of course. Would you not?"

Their body, even satisfied and sleepy as it was, responded, answering him.

"I am saying, kiss her and allow her to kiss you. We will see what comes of it."

"Not ill, my brother," said Twar into his mouth. "I will kiss her, and *you-come-too*."

The brothers kissed then, which was not so absolutely strange to them, and Twar turned his head aside and slept, but Twel slept with his face against his brother's cheek and their coarse hair half hiding him.

She was already there when they came in late the next morning, in the exact middle of the pallet, covered with a rug, her thin arms lying over it, tense and symmetrical. She watched them undress. They knelt over her, and Twar lowered his head and kissed her.

Tasman pulled in her breath. She had thought all day of his mouth, and that he had not answered. In the early evening, she had looked at them as they slept. She knew that Twar would not deny her anything. Yet he had not answered, and Twel had not— why was this so important? But she was romantic and fastidious. In the tales, people kissed, it was the beginning of bonding. And the Sorud kissed her body. She had thought of these things, and not slept, waiting for them.

The Twar's mouth was what made him most unlike his brother. He talked more, ate more. The muscle was larger, more mobile. Laughter was natural to him, his lips moved more in speech, they were thick, like Twel's a little paler than his skin, with a purple-black crease in the corners. Now, as she looked up at him and knew his intent, she was eager and joyous. His mouth pressed over her smaller one, his breath, released, moistened the inside of her mouth. His lips were harder than she expected, and moved and trembled, his tongue suddenly filled her mouth. He drew back, smiled, kissed her again.

They kissed for a long time, and Tasman, less cautious now, touched the darkness of his mouth with her tongue, learned how the lips turned inward, their thick, intricate corners, the slick ridge of his teeth, his tongue and the way it could be soft, thick, hard, pointed. She knew what it could also do, and shuddered with delight, and felt, as he still kissed her, the Twel hand part her legs. When they entered her, Twar's mouth left her mouth, they eased higher, his elbow crooked under her head. This was slow, as always. It made her think of the beach in wind, of sea-return. Their faces, above her, seemed to recede. She was ashamed to watch Twar's face. His eyes were closed tight, and the way he looked was too private. "I am trying not to die. It is so hard, so hard not to die, it is so good." She did not know why she remembered this, or where it came from.

Twel was watching her face, she knew she had only to turn her eyes to him, to meet his eyes, his unreadable gaze. His hand, slipped under her, caressed her where they moved, and he watched her.

She was still uncertain. She did not please them perfectly. "In the romances, it is so easy," she complained.

"They are imaginings, for the most part, tales and fictions," said Twar, stroking her. "Remember, there is no hurry, we are bonded. When you remember that, and become easy, your pleasure will find you, you will not have to look for it."

She glanced from him to Twel, who, his eyes resting on her quietly, seemed to assent but said nothing.

"But I want it to be like it is in the stories. I want to go over when you do, exactly when."

"It is not important. We are like the breath that runs in and out of each other's mouths. There is no right time, there is no best way. It is lovely, too, Tasman, to enter you when you are soft and shuddery sometimes. Tasman, there is no hurry."

So he consoled her, and it sounded very fine, but his face, distanced in desperation, the large changing ways they moved in her, the soft huge ease of their eventual closing, she was still frightened of, she wanted to close with them, then, but could not will it, it eluded her mostly and when they slept, after those times, she lay awake and wondered that it did not shame them as it shamed her, that they had not pleased her perfectly, as it was in the stories.

She walked restlessly in the tower. Twar had kissed her, but she wanted the Twel to kiss her too, and it was as if he would not. On this day they had not come to bed at all, they had remained outside—Twar was divining in the desert, preparing. The dust-motes were shifting, the period of daylight shorter overhead, they were well into the season of Darkening and they were late for it—in their bonding they had deferred everything else. Twel's head must be filled with what he intends to do in Lenh, and that other ruin, she thought, he will not kiss me, when they come home. Kneeling on the rug, she stared at the latticed panes. What she saw beyond them was a bare, modern wall, a shaft of nearly horizontal sunlight crossing it higher up, and part of a corridor. What had they seen then, the Outdead, the people who resembled her, unicephalic barbarians? Other towers? Water?

"Across the street, there, was the House of the Bishop."

Bishop. Biskop. The old race.

"It was cooler then, and Uppsal-a lay on the edge of an inland sea, and there were trees."

"Tell me about snow."

"I do not know what it was, Tasman, forgive me. It is a word they used."

"Did clouds congeal on the ground, because of the cold? Was that it?"

"That is probably how it was. They say it fell. It would be like nightfall, then."

"Not Moonfall!"

"No."

She thought of Twel's gentleness with her. For Sorud Twel, ordinary spontaneous speech was almost always an effort; he avoided it. Yet he spoke with her, and he was always courteous to her. When she was small, his finger lying at her nape or in the hollow of her throat, he spoke very slowly if what he said was difficult for her to understand. And now, his intent eyes—the component of their lovemaking. That gaze that sometimes made her fight against giving in to her joy. How he watched her then! His eyes gleamed when she cried out. And when the Sorud closed, he gasped, she heard him. He had a smattering of pale freckles under his eyes, paler than his skin, and round as coins. And some lines. She had never asked them how old they were. Adults. Even when they'd first seen her, when she was six, in Lofot. Adults even before that, when the Twel had been asked to name her. Adults at her birth.

They were coming in, dusty and sweaty, as she appeared at the tower door. She went to them, clung to them, stale mansmell, dank hang of their garments. She clung as they unstrapped their bundles, and they lifted her across the hall to their room. "Give us water," said Twar, and she ran for it, and squeezed it into their mouths, first Twar's and then more shyly Twel's, and wiped the dust from his eyebrows and wiped his lips. Kneeling over the Sorud, loosing their clothing, she was still disappointed, angry with him. And when the Twar hand reached for her breast she pushed it away.

"Twel Sorud, kiss me," she said, her eyes scared, glancing across his steady look. And he pulled her gently across their body till she lay along his side, and she let herself look at him.

He had turned his head so his face lay close to her face. His arm lay between them, and his hand clasped hers awkwardly, his grip tightening.

"Tasman."

From where she lay, only his face was visible, close and blurred, the eyes gleaming, running into each other. For minutes they watched each other, and, when the Twar hand reached across her, and drew her head closer, she knew it was not the Twar. Twel kissed her lightly, and she could taste his breathing, shallow and fast. Their body swung over her, his eyes never leaving her face, and he kissed her again, harder, his mouth pushed across hers as if he wanted to push it aside, or seal it or erase it, his teeth scraped against hers. They entered her. This was different, fast and fast over with, their weight half-pressed on her, half-supported by his arm clenched beside her head. She had not felt this before, it felt like what she thought being hurt would feel like—she found his look, straining for it, and it seemed angry to her, his lips drawn back, his teeth clenched in a hard black line. Her own anger answered, and she began to resist, but then it was over, she was almost pulled up off the rugs by their hand and they fell against her. Twel's voice escaped him, a wordless sound perhaps also like hurt. They rolled off her and slept—or, if the Twar did not, he also closed his eyes.

12

T here was nothing past the farms, not even a track, but Twel Sorud knew these low dusty hills, and he was a good diviner, so they did not at first have to carry much water. He also taught Tasman the trick of it. The sun rose low and meek in the south and they rested and slept in the hills' shadows or in the trench they had dug for water, against the slight coolness of the under-earth. And walked with the gibbous moon low over them, its creamy light telling them every detail twice over but without depth, so that a gaunt bush, and its shadow, looked exactly the same and they stepped around branch and shadow-branch alike and could not tell which was which. The Sorud bound their foothair around the soles of their feet, but Tasman's bald feet were growing hard: she had outgrown the foot-gloves and refused to consider new ones. She stepped around the rootless balls of cactus by habit now, with hardly a glance.

They had to go south but Darkening increased and it did not get hotter, there was less vegetation and they walked in the long gullies, the moon rolling along the ridges, huge, its details very much like the earth's.

"Did men build there?"

Twel did not answer but Twar said, "Have you not heard the tales? Our race did not, but the Outdead did, it is said."

"I am not yet ready to read those Outdead tales. I have almost begun, I have begun a little. Do you not think, that if you stared at the moon you would see the ruins of their habitations?"

"Ah—they did not live on it. They could not, it is airless. It is said that, with great effort, they may have put things on it."

"When there are two worlds, the moon will be seeded, and the seed of air will grow, and there will be moon's wind on the moon," she recited. "Then, we could live on it."

"Do not think about that. When you look too long at the moon, your feet stumble on the world," laughed Twar, taking her hand.

Twel carried, besides yeast and tools and water, small curious folded sheets as thin as leaves, that he spread out and looked at when they rested. They were tight with little lines of words, on both sides. It was the first time Tasman had seen true book, and she was horrified and fascinated—that he should touch and read this, and carry it on his body outside of Uppsal-a. He did not offer to share it with her, and she tried to keep her eyes averted.

"Sorud Twel is very powerful," Twar had said, and Tasman began to believe this in earnest, when she saw him reading in the desert. As she fell asleep against the twarside, she heard the dry crackle of the pages and knew that the Twel, his head turned from them, was reading by the day's short light.

When they walked he slept often, giving over their body to his twin, and Twar seemed to glory in it, he breathed deeply, arms swinging. "It does not interest my brother to travel for days in the desert or Savannas," he told Tasman. "He prefers to think or to sleep. Our body is strong, but not by his efforts!"

The Sorud lay in a ravine that ran west to east, rising and becoming more shallow as it went. Past its horizon, where it dissipated and spread onto a long hill, larger hills showed, russet in the early twilight of Darkening.

They lay easy against the still cool earth they had thrown aside, their feet dangling over the trench.

"See how she moves, the little snake," said Twar. "She never had to learn it. How early could she have walked? Was what her mothers said true?"

"At one year? She had no understanding, her mothers simply could not let her. They carried her constantly, so they told us. They did not allow Medical Book to see it."

Tasman, across the ravine on the high slope, turned lithely and ran down towards them, then walked more soberly across the level sand. She had emptied the great-pockets of her tunic and the sand-coloured cloth hung slack about her body. Like all the Bering people, she was swart, her hair grew low and close into her features, so her face seemed narrower and steeper than theirs. Fine hair grew forward into the corners of her eyebrows, which were joined over the bridge of her nose to make one straight dark line. "Wide-eyed," her mothers had called the Sorud and all the people of southern Scandinavia, but the wideness was an illusion made by their parted brows, high foreheads and almost hairless temples. Tasman's body was so finely downed that she had a crown high on her spine, and small crowns, like whorls of black sand, on each forearm. The uncut hair on her head was loose almost to her waist, where she had bound it into itself, and tied the ends in a simple knot. But she lacked the handhair, the long strand that grew out of human palms and was their useful tool, and the similar foothair that could protect their feet from burning.

As they travelled, Twel slept often, but Tasman and Twar talked.

"Do you never do the same work?" she asked him once, considering. "Do you work, Twar?"

He laughed. "I keep us going. Can you imagine what it would be like if we were true twins, two like him?"

"But you do not quarrel."

"No, we learned to be friends. It was not always so. We were very quarrelsome in childhood—enemies, really—"

They walked on in silence, Twar smiling. "Ah," he went on, "we were weaned very late because of the fierceness of our natures, we were nearly your age, I think! Twel would not play, and I forced him. Trying to make him run with me, can you imagine it? We were always bruised. He broke my arm, once—"

"Yours—"

"The Twar arm, which I wanted. And he was so stubborn, and mute. I spoke, I guess, four years before he did. Our mothers thought he was perhaps not intelligent. But he listened—ah. He still does that. I knew him, and our fathers did not despair of him."

"Who were they?"

"Sorvar, of Keret, among the makers of knives. They live yet, they were of the first generation who wrote in Book. Small men, wise and silent. I presume, if they *remain-as-they-were*, they do read what Twel writes, and are proud of him."

They were silent for a time as they walked forward.

"We went straight to Book and have been there since," said Twar after a time, quietly. "I accommodate."

"You are not unhappy."

"No, it is not my nature. And this work of his takes us away, to the ruins, he cannot resist, no one knows the things he wants to know, so he had to find them out himself."

Tasman thought. "You give him his way."

"Yes, and he gives me our body." Twar stopped, bent down, and kissed her as they stood. "Shall I wake him? I will waken him, doing this, and this." He laughed softly.

It was strange for Tasman to think of the Sorud as children, with a boy-body, and fighting with each other. They were so harmonious now, despite their great dissimilarity. She remembered her mothers—she had thought them very different, yet they were far more alike, their relationship far less complex. How much the Sorud had to forgive each other! Yet to her

they seemed—surely they were—in perfect sympathy.

They had finally gone to Book, but how had this
been decided? She asked, as they walked, "Twar, how
is it that you gave in?"

"Tasman, we were weaned so that our teeth
could be blackened! It was a terrible time. I said I
would not wean. That if we had to go to Book I would
cover Twel's eyes, break things, or him—in innocence
I threatened whatever I could think of. It seemed to
me it would be like an imprisonment, unbearable. We
were big and strong, we had a bad limp, Twel was as
good as speechless—our mothers were distracted
about us."

"What changed it?"

"Ah—I reasoned, if our teeth were blackened,
and we were adults, what we chose could be freer.
Our fathers arranged for us to come to Uppsal. At one
time they were there. That was the first time we had
travelled. Before we left—" he laughed—"I beat Twel,
I remember that. 'I am going to run all the way to
Uppsal,' I told him. And he let me. As he wanted very
much to get there. He found me of some use."

"I was also denied Book," said Tasman, a romantic pity for the young Twel Sorud rising in her breast.
"I was at Book and could not stay there, the other children were afraid of me. I was at a small one for a time,
later, and learned to read. It was there—"

"It was there we saw you, but you do not remember that."

Tasman thought, Twel longed for Book just as I
did. "Did he not learn to read at all till you were
adult?"

"Ah—he seemed to have learned it, who knows
where? I do not remember him having to learn it. It is
said, that his mind knew the Slavic and the old speech

intuitively, but this is of course the stuff of tales. He learned, but it did not seem to be by a conscious effort. Much is said about him that does not particularly correspond to him."

"What did *you* do at the screens?"

"Sat it out—as I do now. No, I think I applied myself, when I realized there was no one who cared or expected me to. But I believe I slept a great deal. And we roamed in the day, or when I could persuade him."

"But you used both hands and feet, even then, and no people condemned you?"

"We are privileged, and as this worked for us, our parents were relieved. There are none to condemn us, unless we condemn ourselves."

"Were you short-bonded?"

"Yes—to the Say."

She stared.

"Does that surprise you? We lived with them in those years, till we went to stay in Lenh. They are a good deal older than us, though you would not think it. Twelve years, I believe."

"And also, when you came back?" It was hard to ask this, and she stammered.

"Ah—there were many, and none. We have never been house-bonded. Which is a good thing, now you have come to us, Tasman."

13

"Twel." She squatted by his head. It was daybreak, and Twar slept, exhausted, but Twel was alert, turning the leaves of the pages, holding them up one by one, almost translucent, into the coming light.

He turned to her voice and regarded her calmly. "Twel, *our-body* is angry!"

"Your menses is coming."

"I am waiting for it, and not wanting to wait for it. We want to run away from our body." She shivered.

He smiled to reassure her. "That is your impatience. It will come. You know we cannot walk slower, or wait here. There is no water. Sleep well now, if you can, you will feel better when it comes." He touched her throat. "You are not in a fever, your body is not so very angry."

She bent her head into his shoulder in a quick movement, so that the knot of hair struck him across the mouth. "Twel. It does not come."

"It will. Your body is learning. How should it know everything at once?"

caught at the broken top of the ridges, they got up and drank food mixed with careful water, and tied on their bundles.

"Come up over this hill, Tasman, and we will show you the Sheath of the world."

She followed them. The heat was now intense, she had never been this far south. The sand cracked and shifted as they went up the slope, on a long slant, losing the moon for a time in the ridge's shadow, seeing it rise on them like a lopsided, upturned half-bowl, huge, blurry in the heatwaves. The sky around it wavered in brightness.

They cleared the ridge, and looked south.

The Sheath was like the sea. But not flat enough. The surface shone and gleamed in the moonlight, gray-silver and utterly smooth. But not moving. Its undulations were like the standing waves of the rip when the tide poured through the narrows outside the dikes of Lofot. But this surface did not pour. It was utterly without motion, so the reflection of the moon, that would have run and slivered even on the quietest of waters, was fixed. Near and distant swellings distorted this broad path of light, which extended below them and away, slippery and sheening. It seemed as if the whole skin of the world had melted together into agate and obsidian. There were no cracks in the grim surface; its edge, passing below them at the foot of the south slope, was abrupt and thick, like a black wall, its lip sharp as a knife's edge. The desert lay against it in deepest shadow. Along its brink, the shadowline extended away at the base of the ridge, narrowing, curved a little into bays between hills, curved again and disappearing past the most distant points. Above this austere landscape the night air was illuminated to a dusty, dark blue, a visible cloud of particles of moonlight, and far from the moon's edge hung a few large stars, slurred, as if seen through water.

She drew in her breath.

"Don't ask, Tasman," said Twel, interrupting her.

They turned back along the hill on its northern slope, and kept to that valley.

"She says she is sick, that her body is angry."

Twar looked across at her where she sat with her back to them; she was squatting, dawn-weary, her head down, her hands spread out with her fingers under the sand.

"She needs to bleed. We ought to make love, that will start it."

"Here? Twar, we will be in Lenh in three days."

"We'll wait then. If we walk well, we should reach the terminus by tomorrow or the next morning, if we walk continuously."

"Then we would have to carry her, and how can we do that?"

"We can leave the rest of the supplies. Students can fetch them."

Twel considered. "I am sorry for this. It was perhaps not wise to take her so far."

"We could not have done anything else. Our body needs to sleep, let us sleep for a short time now, and then do it."

Twel slept also, for a few hours, and was awake the rest of the journey. Carrying Tasman, they walked in to the terminus in the day's heat, with the sun heavy in the south, the sand scorching even through their foothair, even in shadow.

"Now I can walk," she said, seeing the human walls in the dale, and the traces; but when she tried she staggered, and they carried her to the cars.

Tasman had not known what to expect of Lenh except that she had pictured it more like Uppsal, more inhabited and habitable. It lay in a plain desolate even of grass, and the ground was a waste of rough sand and sharp, small stones the colour of dust. The north part of the ruin was accessible, and close up against half-buried, strange metal walls and towers, modern buildings of clay had been dug down and roofed over —here about a hundred pair of twins lived and studied. Their commerce was to the north, where a broad path, almost a street, extended on past the terminus. There was traffic on it in Darkening, sometimes almost daily.

The Sorud were received formally. Tasman, standing a little behind them, her hand in Twar's, endured the strangers' glances almost without increase in discomfort, too tired to hide her face or scowl. They were shown to a deep room, almost cool, and students came and washed the Sorud's eyes, and Twar washed her eyes, and they drank water.

The Sorud conferred for days with other people. Tasman, leaning in the background, understood only in part. She knew they were planning on going farther, east and south of Lenh, at the height of Kaamos, when it darkened in earnest.

"It is a region of fine dust that is driven with the moon's wind, in tides. And the Sheath is nearer than the ruin Mosc, which lies within the Sheath."

"None of us have been on the Sheath. Perhaps it can be walked on, if the feet are bound up with hair and protected by gloves. But on its hills you cannot stand upright, and if you fall your fingers will be scorched."

"The Sheath is cooler after dark, in Darkening."

"There is no water."

"None of us have gone far into the tidal desert. Can you swim in dust, Sorud? or walk, when the world moves around your waist like water?"

"There would be no landmarks."

"Students among us could go our first and make camps."

"The dust would flow over them."

"But it would turn. There would be high ground, like islands."

Tasman was afraid they would leave her in Lenh, but when they lay down, the Twar comforted her. "You will come with us. This can't be an easy undertaking, and may be impossible. But we can send students ahead, and we will go a short way into this tidal desert and see what it is like, and at the darkest of Kaamos we may take a short walk on the Sheath. More we cannot accomplish this year, unless it turns out to be much simpler than we have been told."

Twel read, and Twar talked with the others and they made plans. At first it was hard to differentiate between the students, but she learned the names of some of them, and a few smiled at her sometimes; there were women hardly older than she was, called Saar, and the Ger, and the Goran, who were very young: all were broad faced and wide eyed, dusty haired and clothed, and they followed the Sorud about. There were also some very ancient twins, inside Book, who spoke very slowly—the Sorud listened to them courteously but impatiently (Tasman could tell this from their body—leaning forward a little, stiff, with small restless movements of their feet or fingers), and the voices of the others slowed also when the old ones were present, as if their thought had stalled and they were all half asleep.

She kept close, in the deep, low rooms, with their strange vertical and horizontal walls and crusted markings, their shelved, open partitions like incomplete walls or steps no people would climb, for they led nowhere, and deeper in, the old landslides of earth and stone being slowly taken away to uncover surfaces as flat as calm water, going off into corridors still hidden and in darkness.

When they were by themselves at night, she slept when Twar slept, deep in the ruin, with Twel sifting meager pages running with words she could not read; she lay across their lap, one arm flung across her face to protect it from the white light.

They made love, but she had not yet bled. "It is her body's immaturity," they comforted themselves. Now Twel laid the papers aside and looked long at her, as he had not allowed himself to do for many weeks. Her sleeping face was thinner and a little sunken, and her body indeed changed, taut-skinned, as if edematous. Their heart suddenly lurched and raced with anxiety, and Twar wakened.

"Look at her," said Twel to him in a low voice. "Is this hysteria?"

After a silence, Twar answered. "It is still possible it is hysteria. That is the only reasonable explanation. There is no one here we can speak to!"

They wept silently, the shame rising simultaneously into their eyes.

"She ate root!"

"Root has perhaps no effect." They spoke in to each others' mouths.

"We who were to protect her."

"Twel, if this can be changed, or hidden."

"They knew my intent in her. She was to be safe with us. It would be attributed to my mind—what they call my unhealth, my curiosity."

"Not now, when she is short-bonded. That is too much shame."

"Do you think they would not? Do you think—"

Tasman woke, staring up at them, her eyes burning. She took hold of their two hands, and pulled them to her belly.

"Listen," she said.

14

They would go north, the Sorud told the others, who believed Twel Sorud had information he needed to discuss in the cities. Perhaps they intended to provide for the poor creature they had short-bonded, so that she could stay there while they prepared and journeyed. Yet, at first the Sorud had said she was to continue with them, and travel with them towards Mosc. The Saar, however, saw her body and wondered, but kept this to themselves.

The Sorud were grim with unhappiness but the others attributed this to their disappointment in not being able to go immediately to Mosc, and they were seen away with ceremony, as for a short time.

It was hot in the cars. They held Tasman loosely. They had not spoken directly to her.

She said, "It was no good for me to eat root, was it? I am not like other women. *Our-body* is not angry, it is inhabited, we are gravid, our children are *inside-us*. What will become of us?"

The first city, Vilpur-i, they reached after a week's walk from the terminus. They met Travellers the first night, and had some conversation with them; but they had seen them from a great distance, at nightfall, and as they approached had waited beside the track, with Tasman hidden behind a bank of sand. She heard what was said, Twar's voice only after the greetings, scrupulously saying only what corresponded, yet saying almost nothing. The Travellers knew of the Sorud, it was obvious, but not of the details in their lives.

After that they walked in short daylight, despite the extreme heat, or when the track was wide and deserted—they did not speak to any others, but let them pass while they rested or slept; they encountered only two other pair, besides those Travellers returning, who passed them.

It was still desert here, low land, the sand moved much and there were no stones, and only vegetation in the hollows—those ashy bushes, and the rootless cactus with its propensity to get under the foot. Tasman saw a snake—it was she who pointed it out to the Sorud—a movement on a hill to the west. Then, they all saw it, as it moved again, going farther away over the hill. From Vilpur terminus they entered the city, and went quickly among bushes and over roofs to a certain building. The Sorud knew this city, Twar told her they had stayed here in their youth—it was a Book connected to Lenh. Tasman ran with them. The night was moonless and very dark when they entered that city, so dark that they could not tell what people were about, and she ran under the Twar arm with her head in his sleeve.

For a time she sat in the small outer chamber and heard their voices, as they spoke with some women there. Twel spoke as often as Twar: she heard his voice break. The Sorud came out with directions, and food, but she did not see the women. They ate quickly and silently, and repacked their bundles, and left Vilpur-i, still travelling north, but a little west, by a smaller track; the Sorud were looking for marks now, and discussed the directions carefully. The nights were very long now and the starlight was deceptive, but they did not lose the track, and reached Sverog terminus in four days, crossing a range of broken hills and meeting no other people.

They travelled on to Savolin in the Savannas, and then to Joensuu, but that trip was a blur of tiredness to Tasman, and she lost track of the days.

15

Joensuu was very small, set in a long north-going dale, a gap between the broken cliffs of a steep little mountain. The cliffs were whitish, some soft and broken and others standing forth in a harder, darker grey, and at the narrowest part of the dale the city was built into them on each side. Over some roofs the sand had sifted down so the houses were almost hidden except for the doors and thresholds. Apart from the main cluster of lights and buildings, over to the southeast where the valley widened, a small house stood for itself, partly built into the eastern cliff of the hill. The nearest light of the city, ochre coloured, just outlined its very low roof that hung as if scowling with old piled grasses and heavy with sand.

Tasman walked ahead of them towards it.

The Sorud had been so silent, so grief-stricken. They had hardly spoken to her on that journey above the necessary things, even the Twar, and it was strange, travelling in this way, courteous as strangers. She attempted to comfort them, with touches and stammered words, but failed in it. When they slept, she lay twelside, clinging to them, and her belly, as if it were separate from her, lay between them, pressed against their heartside so their heart listened, and grieved, and listened.

They had only told her that they were going to Joensuu. Vilpur women had advised them to consult the worldmothers Bogdan-a, and had given them the directions to their house.

They were truly old, the Bogdan-a, with shaved heads except for the silvery plaits at their necks, and great bony foreheads and wrists and hands. Even the black of their teeth was frayed at the edges, and the naked ivory showed at the long roots, where the gums were drawn back. But they saw Tasman steadily, and smiled to her, though they had not received any word of this visit, or even known that she was in the world.

Twar asked, "Did you not know of her?"

And they said, "We did not. But she may enter."

The low rooms were cool, and the earth floor very cool. The Bogdan-a bathed their faces and squeezed water into their mouths, the Sorud's first, as if they knew their need, then Tasman's.

Twar blurted out: "You recognize us or know of us surely, we were directed here from the Book at Vilpur-i. This is the Historian Twel Sorud, we are the Sorud of Uppsal."

The Bogdan-a inclined their heads, then looked at the Sorud directly. Their Twar spoke. "We know who you are now. We will tell you something else—we delivered your mothers of you, at Keret."

They started visibly. "You saw us naked then and you see us naked now!" cried Twel loudly, his voice shaking. "This is Tasman of Lofot. We removed her from that city before her body was grown, she was endangered there through her birthfault, and she has been under our protection from that time." He paused, as if silenced by their quizzical look, then went on—"When she became adult she was immediately short-bonded to us. Certainly she ate root—" again his voice halted, bewildered.

The Bogdan-a approached Tasman and took her head between their hands and held and moved it. They seemed to speak in turns, with long pauses. Tasman could not yet tell any difference between them, or their voices.

"So this is the mind, that has charge of a whole body. And now the body is gravid and well forward in it."

They pulled up Tasman's tunic and felt her belly. "Have you heard your children?" The voice of the Bogdan Twar was disciplined, peremptory, but not unkind.

"Yes, since we left Lenh. They turn like knotted rope."

"Lie down."

The Bogdan-a examined her, while she leaned against the Sorud's side and Twar stroked her as he had before she was grown.

The old women straightened their body. Their hands moved on her belly, listening. Finally they sat back on their heels, said some words into each other's mouths, and smiled. She saw the bits of yellow-white at their gums, as if they had unclean mouths with food in them. They looked at Tasman again.

"This birth will be normal. Your twins are normal."

"You felt their heads, you are sure?" whispered Tasman.

"Yes." They stood up, stooping over and facing the Sorud gravely. "Now you will be house-bonded," said the Bogdan Twel. "There is no shame."

They looked back at Tasman. "You are very young, but in your case, you must have been house-bonded to these men in the course of time. In your case it is not unnatural, because they are and must continue to be your protectors."

"How could anyone dispute this?" said the Bogdan Twar. They faced the Sorud. Their eyes, couched in so many wrinkles that they seemed to be squinting against bright light, gleamed.

"Ah," said the Twar. "We have not been afraid, but we would not have caused this. We would never willingly have had children by her."

"Be easy." The Bogdan-a straightened up slowly, patting Tasman's knee. "Dress yourself. You are to be housebonded."

They remained in the house of the Bogdan-a. From that time, the sorrow of the Sorud lifted; they deferred to the old women in a way that Tasman thought strange in grown men who allowed no one else to command them.

"Is it so, Sorud, what they said, that you would have made me housebond at last?"

Twar answered. They were on the pallet at the back of the house, far in under the hill. "We had not considered this. But we are glad about it. We would never have ceased to protect you, Tasman."

"Is there any tale, where the short-bonded become housebonded?"

He smiled a little sadly. "You will have to write one, yourself."

The old women went in and out, but for days the Sorud remained indoors, and Twar was restless, and Twel closed often inside his own mind. Once, as they sat at food, Twel Bogdan nodded towards them and remarked, "You should go now, and do what you need to do, so that you can return in time to receive the body of your children. Tasman will remain with us."

"We have not demanded this of you," said Twel evenly.

"It is not you, it is we who are saying it. She can be of help to us. It is no sacrifice."

Tasman stared from them to the Sorud.

"Will you go into the tidal desert, and walk on the Sheath of the world, and leave-us here?"

The Bogdan Twel laid a large hand on her arm. "They will return in good time. You cannot go with them, as you are, and it is clear that their minds are not in harmony with this place, they need to go."

Later, in the Sorud's arms, she wept, frightened for herself, though it was she who would be safe. "I want it to be as it was. I want to follow you and stay with you, wherever you go."

"But this will not take so long, Tasman. It is Kaamos already, the end of Darkening, before the world turns to the light. We will journey quickly, and look at these places. If they are so very inhospitable, as people tell us, that will be an end of it."

"But, if you can, will you go on, into Mosc?"

"No." (the emphatic) "We will return to you."

When they left, they told her and the Bogdan-a that they would take students from Lenh with them into the tidal desert. "We will be careful of each other, so that we return. We will leave word at Lenh. You will have a letter from us, if it must precede us, but we will surely be our own letter, and come."

The Bogdan-a did not speak to her between their leavetaking and her falling asleep. But later, she sat up suddenly, calling out, "It is not finished! It is not finished!" and they went to her.

"No, it is not, and you are not to finish it," they said severely, "but hold it in abatement, because they are coming back." Their fingers closed over her arms, hard.

She lay back, tearful and fretful.

"Do not become meek, but remain in this anger," and "You are housebonded," they said.

16

T he Bogdan-a accepted her presence in the house calmly. She kept to the pallet at the far back, but she ate from their bowl. They spoke very little to her, and almost never to each other, and it was not until she was less afraid of them that she discovered they were Tellers as well as worldmothers, and would speak long and eloquently if she asked. Now, most concerned in keeping out of their way, she spent the time angrily wishing for the Sorud, sitting with her back to the light, or lying with her face in the rugs.

The Bogdan-a came and went, mostly silent. Sometimes she wondered if they were true-twins, they conversed so little, and she still had trouble telling them apart; it was only gradually, and in small things, she had an idea that the Twel face was more troubled and the Twar more serene, though both had the deliberate scowl of age. She was unused to reading the look of old people. She thought they moved like children learning to walk, they went so slowly, so she seemed to see the Twel placing one foot, the Twar the other, taking careful thought. They sighed often.

After she had been angry for about a week, and seeing them preparing to go into the city, she asked if she could accompany them.

"Yes, if you remain beside the threshold. We are going to deliver, and they must not see you." The Bogdan-a were tying bundles on their thighs and filling their loose pockets with what looked like leaves. "You are not clean enough to carry any of this. Walk after us."

After that, Tasman went with them sometimes to births, especially if it was day (and they complained that children chose to be born in the heat of the day on purpose, and it seemed so) and no people were out. She waited in the porches, her head against the clay walls. The sounds of birthing became familiar to her. She held her breath at the long moment after birth, waiting for the infant yells, the loud adult laughter. She thought, when she heard newborn twins cry out, her own leaped inside her, answering them.

One night, walking back, she drew level with the Bogdan-a, and said, "Will you soon show me how I am to give birth?"

"You will give birth with great difficulty," said Bogdan Twel. "We will instruct you, but you are small, not yet fully grown, so it will be wise to invite your children early into the world."

"How can you do that?"

"We have medical plants." The Bogdan Twar said, "This is common, do not be afraid of it."

"If the body of my children is not ready—"

"Ah, it will be ready in every particular, only rather puny and thin."

"But if the Sorud do not know of this—"

"Be easy. They know of it. They will come, and we will certainly wait till they are here."

"Bogdan-a, did you truly deliver the Sorud's mothers of them?"

"Yes."

The light in the south was red and pale between the hills. They entered the house in silence, stooping under the shaggy eaves.

She would never by easy with them, but she became more comfortable. It was not as her childhood, north of Lofot, though she was again in hiding. She would not play, she was grown, and to invent stories frightened her, for she did not know what was happening to her housebonded. In abatement, she missed the Sorud with her body, and the presence of new people inside her she sometimes felt as an invasion. She did not know these new twins whom the Sorud had not made in her willingly. And she could not picture them, or their little body that knotted and unknotted itself behind the taut belly-wall, so her skin lumped and wobbled like a snake under sand.

They passed the time with stories, squatting across from each other on the cool floor, the two feet of the Bogdan-a spread and veined and flat, with splayed toes, and with the sparse silvery foothair threaded between them and knotted around their ankles. Tasman stared at their toenails, which were yellow and curved like horns. She forgot the discomfort of her stretched thighs, attending to these new tales.

Twel Bogdan took the speakers' parts: telling, her voice had a surprising range. And to make the voices of men, she spoke directly into her Twar's mouth, lips against lips, so the speech resonated, loud and deep and uncanny. Twar spoke in a rasping monotone.

"Do you ever tell in the city?"

"No, no more. But people come to us sometimes, here, who have remembered us."

And people did come, and listen, and Tasman went in under the cliff and covered herself with the rug on the pallet, so they did not see her. Many of their tales were of the generations, because the women they had delivered of children has told them about their mothers and mothers' mothers. Sometimes the stories were highly exaggerated, fantastic.

They told of a great family of forest women, weavers, all of whom since before they could remember gave birth to only girl twins, and it became finally a city of women, and how of necessity many walked out to be bonded, though they were not Travellers, and perished, and were forgotten, and were dispersed. And when men came, Travellers, they found only one pair left, ancient, crouching on top of a pile of black bones, in a place of bones, who ran behind the bones and peered out when they saw them, and believed them to be monsters with overturned heads (because of their beards) and burnt lungs (because of their speech).

"Away with you," shrieked the Twel Bogdan, when they reached this point,

> *"Away with you, eaters of burned food*
> *Standing on your heads*
> *with your heads between your legs*
> *and your mouths in your foreheads,*
> *and your speech burnt black in your throats*
> *and your knife melted by the burning,*
> *and hanging between your heads—*
> *away with you instantly!"*

—and when the Travellers understood, and tried to show them that this was their ordinary body, the old creatures were truly dumbfounded (because they had forgotten about the body of men) and died of laughter and that was the end of the city.

And they told of women who were milk white, and no one would bond them, till they were brought blind men, and their first children had ruddy skin and seeing eyes. But all their consequent children were white and blind. "We saw this, and we delivered them, and there were many.

"So we charged them to eat root, but they refused, and they reasoned that since the firstborn were perfect, some others would be also. So the firstborn, who were called Dev, were forced to serve their many brothers and sisters, though it was not their fault. They are all dead now.

"Because when the preachers of Moonfall paraded in the market, Dev stood (they were men) all ruddy and strong, with glaring eyes and shouted, 'Nothing is between your hands, before it occurs! Remember us!' This is how they spoke against prophecy, you see. But they were disregarded, although they were perfect. They let no women bond them. They and all the white ones, they are all dead now."

And they told of the great teacher Passerik, in Novaya Zemlya, whose brother, to reward his vanity, loudly contradicted every word that came out of his mouth. The Bogdan-a, imitating male speech, demonstrated this, the Twar intoning in a dull, affectless voice and the Twel sharply negating whatever she said. "So the teacher put an end to it by applying for a new name—he whispered his desire to a Namer when his jealous twin was asleep. And now, whenever his brother shouted out and contradicted him, he was unknowingly crying out his name. Passerik meant *It's not so* in the old speech, but no one knows or remembers that any more. It is only a famous teacher's famous name."

17

O nce, Tasman dreamed, then twice more, waking suddenly in a crouch of terror, her fists at her temples. After those dreams, she began to think that the Sorud would not come back.

It was not a thought or a loss of simple trust. It was a conviction of her body, as if they had been replaced against her will. Sometimes people who went away for a time left a little replica, a doll, inside the threshold, she had heard such tales. In her case, the doll was on its own threshold, in the dark, staring.

The doll leapt at their death,
though the earth was quiet.

At about the time of her first dream, in the south, southeast of Lenh, the Sorud were leaning against the dark wall of the Sheath. Their faces were black, their eyes nearly closed, the lids swollen against the fine sand, which poured past their knees and westward, in small waves. They looked north, and the air was dark, the world fluid and moving. Sometimes the sand broke in a dry froth, close to them, as it flowed around the curve of the glassy wall, and they turned to each others' faces, coughing.

There was said to be a place, before the shelf underfoot steepened and the dust was out of depth, where it had begun to cover the Sheath, and they were looking for this. They had been moving east along the wall, which was still higher than their heads, its knife-sharp edge above them. The wall was so black in the darkness that stars were reflected in it.

"*Allow-me*," said Twar, meaning, Allow me our body, and they began to move eastward again, leaning their back against the wall. "This is like Tasman's tale of the island."

"If you could swim in dust."

"We will reach that place before it rises."

About the time of Tasman's second dream, they were standing against the wall. The Sheath was low enough to see over, and they stood with their arms on its surface, careful of the brink, and stared south, silent with exhaustion. The sand washed past their knees. It had a certain push to it. Though they had tested each step, they had already fallen, foundered, more than once.

The surface of the Sheath here was a slow, almost imperceptibly rising plain, going off into the darkness with no detail except for the watery tracks of two great stars. Twar sighed, and groped into this thigh-bundle and brought out a cloth soaked in water. He squeezed it into his brother's mouth. Twel's lips were cracked and bloody, and he winced.

"We will go only a little farther," said Twar, "so that we will be able to climb up, and can lie on the Sheath and rest."

"Ah, if we rest we may die. We have to turn back to the others."

Twar let his hand slide on the Sheath's surface. It was hot, even now, hotter than the stifling air, though darkness had lain on it for thirteen hours. "You must stay awake for us, then, because we must rest our body."

The sand had risen past their waist now, tugging at them. They went forward step by step, feeling the rim with each hand, testing the hard shelf with each foot, unable to see down past their waist. After some minutes the Twar halted them. Under his fingers he had felt a warp in the rim, and a fine split in it. Using both hands, he loosed the strong braids of their handhair and tied it together, drawing them tight twice, as one would a rope, until it twanged.

"Allow-me."

He jammed the handhair into the crack till it held, and, with a heave, slung their body out of the swirl of sand, till they lay across the edge, their weight on their arms, their legs dangling.

"Now we must be as a snake," he said, gasping, and as they pulled with pain the handhair broke twarside the knot, and they slithered forward. Once they had freed their hands they did not move farther. The surface was almost dead flat here with the slight rise to the south starting beyond them. Twar clean-cut the knot of their handhair with the knife, leaving his brother the present of it, and they lay with their faces in their sleeves and rested, careless of the heat. Behind them, the tidal sand whispered, still rising.

Twel wakened his brother as the dull sun of Darkening appeared over the lip of the world, its long red light spreading over the Sheath like blood.

"Look," he said.

They stared into the light, into a horizon that was, just there where the sun was rising, not smooth but broken and intricate, outlined against the rusty disc like a drawing on a screen—lines, divisions of space, thin, delicate towers. Between two low hills, away in the distance at the edge of sight, its detail sharpened against the sun's swelling ball, visible, till the sun passed above it, rising and rolling to the right. What they had seen faded into the glow. They squinted, rubbing their eyes.

"That is Mosc!" whispered Twar.

"So close—"

They were silent, their body tense almost to pain. At last Twar said, "I know your wish. I acknowledge it."

They had been leaning on their arms but now they got up on their heels, and squatted upright, with their feet on the folds of their tunic. With these words Twar had placed his palm firmly across his brother's forehead, indicating the start of a ritual quarrel. And though it was conducted like a play, it was utterly serious. Twel put his hand on Twar's forehead as well. He said:

"If we return to the camp, and supply ourselves, we can be there before Lightening is well-established. The Goran can return to Lenh, and the others, and bring more people. There is no need to wait for them. You can arrange this." His hand pressed hard against Twar's brow as he spoke the words, and Twar felt their gut knot like a fist.

"No. We are returning to Tasman."

"Women can give birth without men. And only I can do this thing."

"I will not give you the strength," said Twar.

"You will not deny me it. I have always commanded you."

Their voices, spoken into the heat as they stared forward, were quick and low. Now, still with their hands on each others' foreheads, they turned their faces directly towards each other and Twar looked into his brother's eyes. He said:

"My brother, you must in this case be commanded by our housebonding, that binds our body in the body of our children." He faltered almost, facing his brother's stern gaze, but caught an infinitesimal flicker, almost as if Twel had secretly winked. Twel's voice was however stern and implacable.

"That bond was made against our will."

They stared away from each other, as if to look closer was too shameful. The Sheath shone now with an unbearable brilliance.

"She is," said Twar, "besides our housebond, your ward, and by your choice."

"As my ward she is commanded by me. She is in a good and proper place. Our children will live. And she is not just my ward, or just our housebond, she is also my student. That I achieve this is of utmost importance to her. It is her first desire."

"That you see Mosc!"

"Her mind is determined."

"That does not correspond, and cannot be argued. She is waiting for us. Your mouth argues many things. Mine has no need to speak."

"We will send Travellers, as we said, we arranged this, and she will have word of our delay."

"No. She will see our faces. And we will receive into our hands the living body of our children."

At this Twel leaped up precipitously, wrenching them to their feet and tearing the tunic, but his brother had sensed the movement almost as it began, and pulled back his leg, bracing it with his foothair where is slid on the Sheath, and recovering balance. They stood, staring into each other's eyes. Twar jerked his hand away and grasped his brother's head fiercely by the hair at the nape, and Twel copied him, taking hold of his nape-hair and suddenly he did something he almost never did, he grinned at his Twar.

Twar grinned back. "I will not let you do what you are afraid of, and betray her," he said warmly.

Twel answered, his voice gentle, "To go now into the Sheath, and find that city, it is not possible, my Twar, but to plan it is possible. You will begin to make the directions, and perfect them."

Twar shook his brother's napehair in a rough caress, and they dropped their hands. "Let us get off this plate, before we are fried," he said. They stared once last time southward, into the impossible light, where what they had seen, etched in the memory of the retina, seemed still visible at the invisible blazing horizon. They sighed, and kissed each other briefly. Then they turned, crouched on the brink, and dropped into the blowing dust and the Sheath's welcome shadow.

The ritual quarrel had been difficult, because it broke through that barrier of necessary reticence and privacy that was maintained between twins. But they know how to quarrel usefully, and they knew each others' minds. Twel was thus comforted. He could return to Tasman, whom he missed with an intensity that astonished him. He understood his Twar's restless urge towards what was new and violent in the world, and that Twar was yearning to run to Mosc. Because of this the quarrel was necessary, with each taking possession of his brother's shameful wish and speaking it aloud. Yet, their opposition had not been absolute. *I know what you want*, they had told each other, because each knew he wanted it himself. Torn, they were now mended, their purpose single and complete, and they walked strongly back along the base of the Sheath wall, westward, the dust turning and blowing with them around their feet.

About the time of Tasman's third dream, the Sorud were lying in the dust south and a little east of the last camp, which stood on a rise of the hard shelf like an island, the dust breaking against it in small waves. Perhaps they had fallen asleep just as she woke. Particles of dust slid past them, and across Twel's face as he lay.

"Twel, wash my eyes, or I cannot see the camp," whispered Twar. His head, propped on his arm, stared forward, blinded. Twel did not answer.

"Sleep then. I'll breathe for us." Twar undid his arm bundle, and found a water-cloth—the bundle was empty, and the cloth barely damp. It rasped across his eyes. He scrubbed at the right eye until with effort and great discomfort he could see, as through a slit, the blowing desert under the stars, and the camp's low beacon, far to the left of where he had intended it to appear. He shifted and adjusted their prone body till it lay again in line with the light, as he had been doing whenever he was able to see, all these last hours. He put the cloth into his mouth, but could not make it wetter. His eyes were again stuck shut, and burning. He began to crawl forward. Unable to get up and walk, he lifted their body only enough so Twel's drooping head cleared the hard soil under the fluid sand. Their hands gripped at the surface, but only he felt it. He needed his brother's will. "Give me your mind, even in sleep, or we are lost," he whispered. "They will be looking for us before this tide rises." Then, in the midst of a thought, he slept also, his face falling, and dreamed suddenly that Tasman was crouching over them, squeezing cold water from a white cloth into his face, and weeping.

18

T asman, big and restless, moved in the darkened house. Her mind teemed, but her thoughts could not assemble themselves. She was here, surely, but she was also in the south. Daily now the sun breached the horizon, now it rolled along it a short way before it set again behind the treeless ridges. From the threshold, she could not see the path or the terminus, but she could hear the sound of the city, and thought she could hear the cars, perhaps carrying Travellers with a letter. If there is a letter, she thought, they will not come. It will tell of their death.

The Bogdan-a touched her belly, listening to it moving and tightening.

"You are well."

"Will you need to invite them soon, if I am to bear them without harm?"

"Soon, but these twins are small. There is time enough."

One day they told her, "Do not walk without purpose. Sit down and help us." They were cleaning cloth bags and separating plants. Tasman went over to them and they handed her leaves with a brilliant smell, and told her to wipe her hands on them. Swaths of cloth hung along the roof, and the wall pockets were filled with dried leaves, gathered before she had come, at early Darkening. Everything was brown and dull ochre and a dull, lifeless green, even the skin of their arms and hands moving among the plants.

They sighed, almost simultaneously.

Presently the Bogdan Twel asked her, "Are you still looking for the place?"

"Yes."

They had told her she would know where to dig, but she kept changing her mind. It was like a puzzle-tale, where the answer kept altering just as it was discovered. She looked about her. Not a corner, she had thought. Here—perhaps—the thought hardened. The drooping space, the blurry light and dusty smell, felt right and comfortable.

"I will dig here."

The Bogdan-a both grinned. "So we will fall into it daily." Tasman had indicated the space of floor between them and the pallets under the hill at the back.

They assented, however, and she began to dig, squatting, her fingers pulling the earth, extricating tiny stones, then picking away at the edges of their tiny cavities. The trod earth was even harder than she could have guessed. Sweat broke out on her face, slid down her sides. In those days, she worked for hours, and the image of her fingers pulling at the earth was before her closed eyes vividly when she lay down to sleep. Dark ochre in the dark of the room, the pit deepened. She had seen an unfilled pit, in an empty house in Joensuu, the Bogdan-a had shown her it. Hers would be wider than that, and a little deeper, she decided. And the Bogdan-a had said, *Great-pit, first-born/ poor-pit, last-born*, and laughed. They came and went, circling it and complaining peaceably. She carried the loose earth in her pockets and left it beside the north wall.

Now she could complete it and need not stoop; she squatted across it and smoothed its sides with a drenched cloth.

"I wish I had *our-rug* with me, the human hair rug from Uppsal-a."

"You will line it with your own hair. You have plenty. It will be good for you to have it cut. Then your twins will not eat it—it makes balls in the stomach."

"The Sorud will cut it for us," she said loudly, into the pit, her face away from them and the words rang.

"Surely," said the Bogdan Twar.

19

T he day after she had finished the pit, her belly dropped and she felt more comfortable. She stood in the threshold, and her hot reddish shadow swam on the housewall as the low sun peered up under its shaggy brows of grass. Every rootless cactus blown into the path despite her daily sweeping, every grass blade piercing out of the sand, even every little tilted stone shone with its own importance and cast its own little shadow proudly across the earth.

Small day, make bright
the visible world.
Small day, shorten your shadows,
stay with us.
Be swollen, stay with us.

Twar had told her, when she sang this to him a year ago in Uppsal-a, that it was indeed a northern song, for in the south people did not long for light, but for darkness, they preferred darkness to heat. But Twel had said, "It is an old song. In the old days, even in Lightening, the world was cool."

Her belly leaped as she saw them coming, stretched up as if to take her by the throat and prevent her breathing. She knew them instantly by their walk, yet they walked very slowly. She ran forward, calling out, and just as their shadows touched her feet, the water gushed from her.

"Bogdan! Bogdan-a!" the Twar shouted aloud, but his eyes were bound, and Tasman, lifted up to them and her ears stunned by his loud cry, saw tears running from beneath the filthy cloth. How very black their faces were! She tasted their rough skin, their smell, bitter with earth and salt. It was she who half-supported them, laughing and crying, into the house, and she helped the Bogdan-a squeeze water into their mouths and over their necks and faces and breast and hands, and wipe their hands and faces. The Bogdan-a drenched them, as for a great celebration, and the dirt from their body ran in muddy rivulets on the floor.

Then her belly fisted as she knelt over them, and she straightened up to accommodate it, and looked into the faces of the Bogdan-a. The Bogdan Twel nodded, and her sister said, "We are listening. This is indeed a day for the Tellers, a folded day, with so much content in it."

The house was full of movement and voices. The Sorud ate, while Tasman crouched with her back pressed in against their seated body, and felt their breath and watched their great hands take food. She felt their heavy presence. This was real, the real weight and smell of them, and again her belly clenched like a fist. She took their two hands, and wiped the food out of them as well as she could, and laid them on her belly.

"Listen, my Sorud."

"I am very glad," said Twel, his mouth pressed into her hair so it muffled his words, "I am very glad we have come back."

Tasman walked about, crouched, returned to them where they leaned, in the centre of the house, in the drying mud among the scattered pockets and leaves and bowls.

"Is Twar asleep?" she asked, pressing in under their arms.

"No," Twar answered. "We need to sleep, but we can sleep later. We will watch with you. But I am not good at watching, the dust has got into my eyes."

"The Bogdan-a will clean them for you," Tasman said. She pulled at their ragged tunic, sniffed their chest.

"Sorud, I am wet and bursting. But it will take a long time. Sleep now—better than later—" she pushed them back, and tucked their headsleeves under their heads, and looked into their ravaged faces. "I am so tender now towards you," she cried out. "I thought that Travellers would come and tell me a letter, that you were dead or lost. I hardly dared look out for you, I was afraid I would see Travellers instead."

Twel smiled at her, and she bent and kissed him, then Twar, impetuously. As she sat up Twel reached out and rested his hand on her belly, and turned his face into his brother's neck, and slept.

The Bogdan-a took Tasman's clothes away, and washed her. They listened to her belly.

"Are their heads well down?" Tasman asked. For she had picked up what she felt was considerable knowledge about birth, in these months.

"Yes. Feel them."

"They are leaping."

"They will crouch soon." "You are limber, you will do well."

But Tasman knew about firstbirth, if not from them because they would not deliberately worry her, from her mothers, and from small remarks of the Bogdan-a, overheard after firstbirths in Joensuu. So she heard in their reassurances—despite their long practice in the calming of frightened women, a shadow of uncertainty. She went over to the pit. "When the Sorud waken, I will have them cut our-hair."

Unknotted, undone, it was a massive swath Twar's hand could hardly hold. The Twel cut it roughly across the crown of her head, while she knelt, and it fell across the Twar hand.

"How light and small we are now," she said uncertainly, her fingers touching the ragged crown that felt like stiff grass. She took the hair from them and retied it, and bound the cut end also, into a thick, gleaming knot. Then she laid the swath in the pit, snaked, so it formed a glossy pillow.

Looking into the pit, in the dim room, seeing her shorn hair lying there, she suddenly knew that this was real, she was indeed to give birth, to welcome a new body and new minds into the world.

117

"This is no Lofot pit-pool," said Twar admiringly, as his hand felt into the pit, touching the hair.

"No," said Bogdan Twel. "In the Interior we do not have so much water to spare that we can allow children to swim into the world."

"Do you know our Pit-pool tale?" asked Tasman, sitting back on her heels.

"Yes, or a version of it, but that is not a tale to tell at a birth."

In the tale, Tasman recalled, the women who were about to deliver went into a large, natural pool in the forest, and deliberately drowned themselves—because they were abandoned and in despair:

> *But the birthed babes,*
> *trailing the placenta like a long bait,*
> *squirmed towards shore.*

"My mothers told it to me in Lofot." Tasman's eyes suddenly streamed, as from an old infection breaking out years after the body has thought itself well. The Bogdan-a saw this, and came close and embraced her, as her belly again fisted. *"Worldmothers be my mothers,"* she whispered.

"We *are your mothers*," they answered in unison, peremptorily, but their touch was kind.

She was dreamy between the times her body clenched and loosened. She lay in the Sorud's arms. The Bogdan-a wiped her mouth and her body. She roused herself and helped the Sorud wash, and then clenched again, her body tight against their wet nakedness.

"Shall we invite the body of our children? Shall we touch them?" asked the Twar, softly, as they came closer. But she moved away from them, abashed, and went to the door and crouched there. She saw the great moon leaning on the south of the world. Its bigness answered hers. It was blurred strangely, a cast of light across it, erasing details, and when she blinked and looked again it was no clearer. Tranquil and Imbrium still showed, sad eyes:

The moon looks over his shoulder,/he regards his path,/ he is sad / he is going where he does not want.

In the house the Bogdan-a crouched with the Sorud, watching her.

Tasman labouring: her brows contracted as if in pain, her nostrils flared, her mouth pulled wide, her teeth bared. And at ease, waiting: her eyes half-shut and her lips parted as in lovemaking, dreamy and soft. She stayed at the pit now—in it or over it—she lay across it, her belly pendent, the Sorud grasping her arms. She crouched: there was blood on the cut coil now, and the Bogdan-a, touching her, guided her fingers to touch the presenting head of her twins—it felt strangely malleable and soft, yet this was what pressed her thighs apart almost unbearably, as if it were a great rock. Twel Sorud squeezed water across her mouth and eyes.

"*It is not pain, it is joy,*" Bogdan-a continued to repeat, meaninglessly. Tasman, who could not remember pain before this, would have called it, if not pain, something more appropriate than joy—anger, perhaps, or murderous hate.

Her children's body was splitting her apart, surely; she would be lame if she lived—she had seen lame women in Lofot.

Now she lay back against the Sorud as she squatted over the pit. The Bogdan-a faced her, their hands reaching for her children. She felt as if time had stopped, as if she would labour in this hot, low house, over this pit whose edges were already crumbling away, forever.

"Nothing is happening! I am tired out!" She began to shake and she could not stop herself.

"They are at the threshold, they are knocking," said the Bogdan Twar calmly, and her sister suddenly shouted, "Look at us!"

Their faces blurred and ran out of focus, fierce with age.

"Your children are tired. Release them into the world," went on the Bogdan Twel, still loudly. At her words Tasman's body fisted again, desperately, and the Sorud gripped her under the armpits; she could feel Twar's mouth and teeth against her cropped head. The pressure increased, like heat, like scalding, as if she were to be consumed. Past it she saw the Bogdan whispering into each other's mouths. Something turned and fled away violently down a long, distant path. She yelled. The Bogdan-a grasped the Sorud hands and pulled them down to receive their children. She leaned back, sliding from them over on her side. Everything was black, the reddest of blackness. Her voice yelled again, and stopped. She heard their voices, at a great distance.

The Twar saying, "What is it? What is happening?" and the Bogdan-a, "Cut this," and "Wrap it, it lives," and Twel, in the clearest of tones, like a voice carrying across water, "Did you know of this?" and, "You told us otherwise."

The Bogdan, speaking quickly over each others' voices: "At the time you went away we did not know it." "Only later did it seem." "Did it become apparent." "Reach down your hands!"

The second body slid out, easily—slippery and gray-black. Tasman saw this one; in silence her hands dragged it up her belly, where it lay still, and then suddenly screamed, and its cry was answered by the one in the pit—two voices—

"Two voices," she heard the Twar saying, bewildered, in sorrow, his hand moving tentatively across the body of the one on her breast, closing over its single head. For an instant Tasman believed that great hand would tighten there—crush it—

"Two voices," repeated the Bogdan-a, their own voices back in control now, matter-of-fact. "Come, Tasman, we will swaddle your children in your hair, and you can look into their faces. Their body is—their bodies are—that of men."

They wrapped the babies together and laid them on her breast, and with a last expulsive clench the placenta fell into the pit.

"Two voices," whispered Sorud Twel, and she saw that he was weeping. She stared into her sons' faces, felt their shuddery breath as they cried.

"When we apprehended this, nothing could be done," said Twar Bogdan. They moved about heavily, fetching cloths, washing Tasman, binding her. "Take her with her children to the pallet, she is tired."

The Sorud carried her, clumsily, as she held fast to the babies, and laid her with them in the cooler alcove under the hill. They leaned beside her. Twel staring at the babies, so well wrapped in the bands of her hair they looked perfect, as if they shared one body. Twar moved his hand over their wet faces and their mouths turned after his fingers blindly, trying to suck them. One skinny arm was bent and the hand fisted at one of the faces, and he parted the tiny fingers and felt a vestigial hairless palm. The little hand clutched his index finger.

Twel spoke: "As I love you, I love them, Tasman. But our heart is breaking. The Bogdan-a said nothing to you, that would warn you of this?"

She answered him slowly, as if her mouth had to relearn speech. "I knew they were afraid, but I thought it was because of my youth. They said nothing. They said, 'Your children are well,' and 'You are well'—nothing else."

The Sorud backed away and went into the other room; she saw them stooping and walking, filling in the pit over the afterbirth, and she could hear the noise of the earth being thrown down.

She loosened the babies, and suckled them, and her heart beat steadily with tiredness and wonder. There had been no laughter, because there was no joy. Yet her sons lived, they were small and thin but she saw that their bodies were whole, the first one a little larger and darker in colour, a little louder in his voice. "Yet you waited till you heard your brother, before you drew breath," she said to him, and unreasonable, unstoppable laughter welled in her, and pushed out of her, and she laughed, and pulled them against her, and slept, the dirty swath of black hair, caked with earth and blood, tangled across her body.

When she woke, the babies were sleeping, and she lay still, hearing the voices of the Bogdan-a in the larger room.

"—or fragments of one, that did not live."

Twel said something.

"No, it is possible they did not themselves know it, and some worldmothers, or her fathers, disposed of it."

Twar said, "Her fathers went away at her birth. They are dead."

"They may have burned that other one in the desert."

Twel said, "It does not signify anything."

There was silence in the house. The Twar broke it finally.

"Tell us, Bogdan-a, what did you intend, if we had not returned?"

"Had we received word that you were dead, we would have allowed them death. We were not certain you would come back, though Tasman trusted you, we have lived a long time."

"And without word?"

"We did not know what to do, we would probably have allowed them death."

"Because they resemble the Outdead?" said Twel, his voice carefully expressionless.

"We were sure that both would perish. It is not the habit of the birthfaulted to demand life."

"We knew nothing of this until too late," went on the other Bogdan. "They lay face to face in her belly, we felt their heads. The one lay somewhat behind the other. Then, they turned around."

Again, there was silence. When Twel spoke, his voice was distant and courteous.

"We will go from you soon, Bogdan-a. Our difficulty will not continue to be yours." He had turned away, and it was hard for Tasman to make out what he said, the babies whimpered, and she could hear nothing distinct. He spoke for a long time, very slow and quiet, his words interrupted by long pauses. When the Bogdan-a replied, their voices were resigned, softer.

"We will not live to see that, Sorud Twel." "Or to have to be persuaded."

Joensuu to Lofot at Esmenvar in the street of jas-
mines, 442 Lightening, the third month, to our
mothers.

Our mothers, this is to acquaint you with and
assure you of our generation, as is required of
us. We, Tasman, of Uppsal-a, living in the city
of Joensuu in eastern Scandinavia, have given
birth to living, male twins, sons of the Sorud to
whom we are housebonded. Their name is
Avskel (meaning, the divided ones).

Our mothers, we are well and our sons are
well. You will wonder at the words of this letter, but though we ate root we were not prevented from receiving children. In face they
are like the Sorud, that is, broad and not swart,
but they darken, especially the first, who was
least dark.

We have had many adventures, which Sorud
Twel assures me you will one day read in Book
in Lofot—but not now. The Sorud have walked
on the Sheath and have not been harmed,
except that the Twar is blind, but his sight is
returning, strong light he can see sometimes.
We live at the house of the worldmothers
Bogdan-a at the edge of the city. They delivered the mothers of the Sorud, and they deliv-
ered-us as well. When this letter is told you,
however, we will have gone away.

Our sons greet you with words before words.
Greet the Fa, and tell them this. The Sorud
greet you. *Remain as you were when we took leave*
of you, so that our minds, and your minds, are in
harmony with the world.
Tasman.

three

20

The Avskel were now eight years old and lived with Tasman and the Sorud south of Novaya Zemlya in the low forests. Her twins were unweaned, yet she had become pregnant four times since the world learned that the moon was seeded. None of these children lived—they had been born too early. They were unicephalic like her and her living sons. She was again pregnant.

In this year (450), the dense clouds that had covered some parts of the moon for eight years had partially cleared, and it was seen that the centre of Imbrium, that great blind vale, was dark blue. No people knew what this meant. Serenitatis, also, was changing, and between them ran a corridor of deepening blueness, so people said it was not water, because it did not change or shine or follow the lowest contours. It was surely vegetation. But in the common speech they called it the canal of the many bridges, as they spoke of the Sea of Quiet and the Sea of Rains.

Twar Sorud had continued blind, and his mind darkened in adversity; he would not permit Twel to direct him, but when the Avskel began to walk about, the first-born of them, whom they called Atwar, spoke first and showed him whatever he could, and so, if the Sorud walked out, Atwar would sit on the Twar's arm, and chatter to him. But later Atwar walked beside him and took his hand. Betwar, the second-born, was larger and stronger but less quick to speak.

These years had not been easy either for Tasman or for the Sorud Twel. There was no Book nearer than Novaya Zemlya and the time Tasman had intended for intense study was spent unwillingly without access to words. But Twel taught her the Old Slavic, and he showed her what true book he had with him from his journeys. Her memory was almost faultless and she learned much, sitting across from anyone who would tell her tales, repeating with the concentration of a Teller.

When the season of Darkening after Twar's blindness had come and gone with no improvement to his sight, the Sorud had gone north to Novaya Zemlya. But at the Medical Book there they could not heal him.

Already the mood of the world was sweetening, for at their arrival the city was decked as for a festival, and the full moon in daylight, blurry and glowing, was the subject of every song and tale. Twel resigned himself to the pressure for information to be read into Book, ensuring only that it was a record of fact, and not speculation or prophecy, that was entered. There they saw their fathers, but from a roof, hidden, because their fathers' minds had closed in age and they would not have recognized their sons.

When the Sorud returned to Tasman and the babies, Twar sang her a song he had heard in the great market:

> *The moon draws near to us*
> *and hides his face*
> *the cloth is raised across the windows*
> *of his eyes*
> *we are afraid of his radiance*
>
> *In the forest below*
> *lives a woman, risen from the Outdead*
> *her face is his face, her voice is his voice, she says,*
> *Do not be afraid.*
> *I will not hurt you.*
> *She repeats this.*

Twel, as Twar sang, reached out for and touched the face of their housebonded, and in the silence when the song was ended, smiled sadly and said, "The world knows you are in the world, it is up to me to see they begin to be kind to you."

"Will we be able to return to Uppsal?" she asked.

"Perhaps."

At the next Darkening, the Sorud had gone away again, and in the subsequent Darkening, they brought students back with them, who helped to dig further houses and another well. In their eyes Tasman saw a new, shy friendliness. And they were kind to the Avskel, who had begun to walk before they had understanding, and had to be watched constantly. There were the Bering twins, women, who stayed with her, and she became friends with them, but when they had told her everything they knew, the days dragged.

They called the place Siya, which was an old name, but they did not know exactly where that city had been, as there was no trace of it.

The Twel brought true book back from Uppsal. But the Twar had not been healed. At Lenh, more true book were found. Twel and the students had entered it in Book, with Twel's commentary around it, and Twel brought the true book back with him.

Mosc was written of in this book, and a city called Tchern. "It is there, in Mosc, we may find word of this ancient seeding, what it was and what was expected of it."

But as yet no one had been able to cross the Sheath to Mosc. There were eager, wild students at Lenh. They wanted to make a tunnel under the Sheath. Others spoke of a natural tunnel, an ancient river-bed, and searched for it in pictures that had been found.

Some more sober plans were being laid. Twel supervised them, they went forward at each Darkening. Twar, with his knowledge of the desert, was of more use than he had dared expect, but his mind was full of lassitude.

Though it was not his mind, but his brother's, that suffered, Twel felt their body's infection intensely. He did not know how such an anger, as now was locked in the Sorud breast, could be sustained, and he could not tell any longer how it had begun, or how it could be healed. It was as much his as it was his brother's, for it constricted their lungs equally, it clenched at their stomach. His throat ached with it when they lay down, and his breath was short with it when he awakened.

Yet it was not the anger of sickness, toward which men ought to be attentive. It was mind-anger, and wrong. The calm of what he now thought of as his youth was gone as if forever, his power seethed.

It was not his brother's blindness as such, it was the harm of it; surely it was Twar's despair that had taken over their body, and Twar would not allow him to speak of it, or to lead him, or to show him ordinary tenderness. In the day Twar lay with his face turned to Tasman's, but he would not speak closely with her either. And when she lay beneath them, it was his strength that thrust into her body, but his mouth would not cry out.

When Tasman had given birth to tiny dying twins, only those times, did the knot loosen in tears; over those limp bodies that could rest in the palms of their hands, their grief erased everything else. But quickly it grew again—the painful tightness in the chest—and the brothers had to share it, whoever was to blame.

Tasman accepted their condition, which seemed to her a natural sadness, and forgave it. She had not ceased to expect the Twar's eyes to improve, that he saw light ("It is always light," he had once said) seemed to her a good sign, a prophecy that the light would eventually take shape and form. When they lay down to sleep she licked and licked his closed eyes, willing them to heal. Towards Twel she felt shame, and her own longing to learn was an itch in her. She wanted to be perfect, and the way they lived was too primitive, what she learned was not enough. In her head she carried the story of herself, word perfect, and it spread. As her sons grew, she sometimes whispered it to them, and in this way they learned of her generation, her childhood, the shore north of Lofot and how the Sorud had come and taken her away.

So her mind moved in words, and when she was sick these comforted her. The bearing of children to no purpose enraged her body, and she was afterwards in a fever many days. And now, at twenty years old, her face was unlined but haggard, her eyes a little too deep-set under the single black browline. The hair she had cut at her sons' birth was dense and long, but matted and reddish (for the earth at Siya did not nourish her perfectly) and she wore it close over her shoulders like a sleeve.

Now, on a night well into Lightening, they sat in front of the houses in the clearing and waited for the nearly full moon to rise above the trees. Atwar lay on the earth at the Sorud's feet, on his back, grasping a dusty footsole and working out a thorn. Tasman leaned at the Twel side, and Betwar leaned into her lap half asleep, his mouth at her breast, occasionally squirming and sucking at it. At the door of the house to the east, the Bering twins sat back against the lintel, passive, and before them the students, Avra and Goran, lay on the earth, talking softly.

"Mar, it is out." Atwar lifted a skinny finger, then wiped it on his sleeve. He squeezed the puncture, and licked his bald footsole thoroughly, his body knotted. Then he stood up and went to the Sorud, and leaned into the Twar's arm.

"Fadel, it grows light there now, can you see that?"

"Almost, my little son."

"I will tell you, and then you can see it."

The edges of the low trees were becoming clearer in detail now, as the moon neared their tops, the sky bright cobalt. The last of the moon's wind pushed through them, a rush, a whispering. It passed.

"Now, Fadar." Atwar took the Twar's head between his narrow hands, and turned him to face the southeast, exactly there, where the rim of the moon rose over the highest fronds of spiny palms and wild, fruitless banana trees.

They watched intently. At first it looked disappointing—white and blurred, but as more came into view they saw that the face of the moon was now only sparsely clouded.

"It is blue, Fadar, the seas and the canal are showing. The canal is wide, as wide as my finger, and it has a black edge, jagged, at Imbrium in the south, like a well wall, and the whole of the Sea of Quiet is blue with cloud across it—"

"Would it not be terribly hot there, Fadel?" asked Betwar, who was now wide awake. His voice was slow and serious.

"Terribly hot, perhaps—" said the Twel, "in that long day."

"But under the blue trees—" said Atwar.

"There, it would perhaps be cooler."

Twel turned to his brother, whose face was intently raised, whose open unseeing eyes were milky in the moonlight that lay across his broad cheeks and forehead.

"Twar, how could this have been achieved, and no word left for us?"

"Ah, they hated us."

Tasman said, "I believe there is word, in Manj'u, in that Book."

"Until we know we can only guess," said Twel, "and that is useless. Nothing from those times has yet been found. There is nothing but these Moonfall songs, and they are too recent. Yet there must be predecessors. We have to keep searching."

> *He went by the south*
> *and burnt his mouth,*

—said Atwar suddenly, and laughed.

"That tells us nothing," said Twel.

The blue was the blue of the far hills towards Novaya Zemlya, the deep forests behind them where the tide ran miles in among the stems. Marsh blue, and the crater Chmedes' great rim black as the Sheathwall. Imbrium was patchier. The children saw clearest of all. Atwar and Betwar saw gold rock patches in its blueness, and the edge of cloud and its shadow, slowly passing. They saw the bluing of smaller seas, Vaporium, Nectaris, and Crisium, and the Lake of Death like a well with its lid off in daylight.

"Do you see it, Fadar?" Atwar persisted, again turning Twar's face a little.

Twar smiled. "It was, a little brighter, there."

"Fadar, one day, let us go walking in the blue forests."

"I would like that, very much, my little one."

The boys were weaned at the end of that Lightening. Tasman still carried children, and they moved, and she began to hope she could keep these ones comfortable until they were well grown. So the Sorud stayed, Twel sending the Avra to Lenh, with minute instructions. Towards Kaamos in the middle of that Darkening they received visitors.

First, Travellers came, running, their faces black with weariness. They came from the east, but had stopped at Severod and turned aside, because they were looking for Sorud Twel and Tasman.

The first who saw them were the Avskel. They were playing at the edge of the clearing, and the Travellers stopped in their tracks at the sight of them, and stood silent. Atwar called loudly, and the Sorud came out of the house, and so did the others, and went over

to them, but Tasman stayed in the doorway, and
waited.

She stood in her maturity, looking across the
bright, hot earth with its threads of brown grass, and
the first well, still half-picketed with sticks they had
set up when the Avskel were small, with the yeast-
yard around it, and the sparse forest beyond with its
almost-black shadows, where the adults stood smiling in a shy group, and her sons moved about them
restlessly, dark naked bodies and sunbleached hair.
Weaned now, they were no longer hers to mouth and
roll with in play, their taste must be forgotten as they
must forget hers, as their bodies grew. And the children inside her, who had begun delicately to knot and
leap, who would perhaps replace this loss. The others
had not stayed so many months, they had all been
girls, there had not been time even to dig a pit, suddenly they had wanted out, had escaped from her.
They had not so much died as just drifted out of
being, the tiny bald hands dropping on the long, fin-
ger-thin wrists. Perfectly finished in her image, yet
they could not breath or cough or cry.

Something was changing, and though she had
been in hiding now for eight years, she was known
and not threatened. She sensed a new sureness, as if
the heat from the clay lintel, pressing along her spine,
were urging her to stand straighter, to meet these
strangers with pride rather than shame.

They came, walking between the Goran and the
Sorud, their hands spread empty in the formal ges-
ture, their faces very closed, courteous and austere.
They were of the Sorud's age, but as easterners, with
sleek, flattened hair and very straight, shallow-set
eyes. Their Twel spoke first.

"We are carriers of a letter for the Twel Sorud and his Twar, and their housebond Tasman. It was told us by Travellers from the east who run between Turuk and Pur. And it was told them in another language and in another form, and its directions were to the Book of Turuk, where it was received and changed into your speech."

They squatted, their eyes fixed on Tasman's. "Give them water," she told Betwar, who was closest to her, and he went off to the well. She took the cloth from him and herself squeezed water into their mouths, and wiped their faces. Then she drew back, so that they could enter the house, and followed them, and the others came after them.

Their Twar had a loud, rather sharp voice that filled the low space of the house. "I am repeating the first letter, as it was before it changed," he said, and began.

It was said in later years that Twel Sorud intuitively understood the words of the alien tongue, which the Traveller called out aloud and without expression or pause. He continued in the common speech:

Fu-en the Book, the men who read Book and those who read Book in Turuk. Lightening 449, Darkening. This letter is told to the people.

Know that in the Northern straits, word has been received from the Book at Manj'u, that the Sheath is broken and the moon is seeded, and that his seed has given fruit. The tide of the Sea of Peace has burned up and run under the Sheath of the world and there is a Lake like a mirror and in its glass the expression of the moon is made clear and it is benevolent. What was begun by the ancient race is perfected. The moon's wind is perfected on the moon and moves

136

under the surface of the dust as the sea runs under
the Sheath of the world. The wind on the moon has
become water, and the water wind, and in it the cold
seeds have restored themselves after three thousand
Darkenings. As this is told to you, the depressed
land of the moon is receiving the fruit of the seed.
Gods did not do this, but men who are now dead,
when they saw the shoulder of the moon lean
towards the world. They did not forgive us, or trust
our race, and therefore they sought our death, but
they could not prevent what they had made. They
wrote it in Manj'u, in the First Script, which is pre-
served at the source of the Lake at the city of Fu-en,
in a script that is lost but not lost.

What is happening is happening according to the
script. The script ceases at the end of the year of
greening. There is a screen the size of the single head
of an ancient man. Only he can make this journey.
Yet who will mutilate themselves for this unutter-
able purpose?

At this point, the Twar teller broke off suddenly,
and his brother, in a slightly quieter voice and speaking even faster, took over.

From the Book of Turuk, this letter was corrected
and redirected. To the city of Uppsal, Sorud Twel.
The head is the head of a woman. The journey is pos-
sible. There is a woman in the western forest, and
the Sorud Twel knows where she is to be found.
Whatever is not understood, will be understood,
and the Teller of this letter will show her the way.

Sorud Twel prepared the Travellers a letter to
speak in the east, saying that a journey into Mosc was
to be attempted in the next Darkening "where we will
perhaps find the rest of the script you have spoken of,

and other things that were written in those days. And I will write these into Book at Lenh, but I will not write anything but what I find, and what is now seen." Twel said this because he was determined to prevent Moonfall being written. He asked Tasman also, so she could not refuse, to tell a letter to be carried to Manj'u. But she only said,

"I am that woman. I did not determine what is required of me, but we will come to Manj'u with our household."

When the Travellers had learned these letters, they went away.

21

L ater, when it was cooler, they took leave of Siya, with a large group of people who had come down from Keret to accompany them, and travelled to Lenh. The houses in the clearing were closed, their doors filled in and the wells marked and covered, and no one remained there. At Joensuu, Tasman went aside with the Sorud to visit the Bogdan-a. But the house under the cliff was changed: young boy twins came out, staring. They lived there in short-bond with other worldmothers. The Bogdan-a were dead.

Tasman, however, received strength from the shape of the room, and they stayed there two days, and the worldmothers touched her, and told her that her babies would surely live.

"Then I think they are sons, for daughters I have been unable to carry to term."

So they went on from city to city, and people joined them and went with them. They carried Tasman when she was tired, but she mostly walked, feeling stronger after the time in Joensuu.

At the beginning of Kaamos they reached Lenh, and she gave birth behind the Sorud's apartments, in a pit of soft soil, on a night with no moon. Her babies were girls, and divided like her sons, each with a separate body, but they had two voices, and this time she laughed with joy, the Sorud laughed with her, and the Avskel, sleepy, crouched against the roof, crept over and touched their sisters wonderingly. At the seventh day they were named Liv, which means, life.

When the babies were four weeks old, and it seemed they would surely live, Tasman told a letter to her mothers in Lofot, but before it could have reached them, word came of two floods in that region and all along the Barents coasts, the second of which had not receded, but had remained, and made the city uninhabitable. There had been no natural catastrophe in modern times, tidal increase had been gradual and accommodated, and the moon's wind also had only grown strong in this generation, and had not varied in its acceleration. But around the time of the birth of the babies, it began to strengthen very much, and become erratic, and it was not pleasant even in the heat to go up and meet it any more, for it moved heavily, and carried masses of stinging dust into the city from the tidal desert, and disrupted the irrigation at the farms, so people stayed indoors when it passed over.

Because of this news, Tasman's mind was turned from her childhood and the place and people that had not *remained as they were*. She lay in the apartments with her face towards the east, and suckled the Liv, and was aware of how the house of her mind had changed, as if a door were filled in behind her, and a door opened towards the east, with the moon filling it.

The Avskel ran with their fathers into the old Book. There, the way to Mosc was made ready—in the fifth month of Darkening it was to be attempted. At this time, more people came from Lofot and the coasts into the cities of Bjast and Uppsal, not Travellers but homeless people. And in Uppsal, a certain man with a mute twin rebraided their thick, hempish hair, and wiped his brother's mouth, and walked across the street to the house occupied by the Say, and kicked courteously on the door.

22

There was no underground river or riverbed into Mosc. The journey was made to the Sheath's low point along a ridge now almost bare of dust, the first group of students covering themselves during the moon's wind with rugs held down by their bodies. At the edge of the Sheath, they bound their handhair thickly around their hands and fingers, and their foot-hair around their footsoles, and cut and tore some of the rugs and bound their feet and hands with these also, and set out across the Sheath. They brought a long rope with them, of fatted human hair, because the Sheath had no footfast. About halfway to Mosc the ground began to rise. The moon's wind passed and carried them, as they had calculated, across this ridge, but the Goran could not follow, having no purchase, so they sent water back to them along the slope, and left them, but there was one more slope which they could not come over, though it was also very low, so they waited for the next wind.

The second group dug camp under the Sheath wall and to this place much water was brought, and buried, because on that shelf they could not find any well. The Sorud joined them and went out on the Sheath with that group. They reached the Goran but they could see from a distance that the body of the Goran was dead, and when they came up that it was burned, from the heat of the Sheath's surface. But the rope over the ridge had purchase, and from then on they could use it and follow easily. Mosc's towers now rose close and in great detail. They were like the lines of a city drawn on a screen, and nothing filled in. They were mostly verticals, and were joined by straight horizontals, and with the topmost joins curved like the moon's limb or a smooth, steep hill.

When they reached Mosc, they found the first group just inside the first line of towers, where a horizontal crossed a the level of the Sheath and emerged near a far tower. Because of the Sheath's slight slope, it rose there to near men's height, and in its small shade the students were gathered, lying close together in each others' arms. The rope of human hair was tied around a shard at the foot of a vertical, and around each of their bodies under the armpits. On this terrible scene the sun rose and journeyed briefly across the southern sky, and the living, who had found them, crouched in the shade with the dead. Sorud Twel searched their tunics and bodies. They were not burned, but as if dried out and brittle. When the sun set, he said to Twar, "Let us go into this city, and look at it." Speech was a greater effort than he had expected. No one had spoken, since they had reached the towers.

They walked along a horizontal that was near the Sheath level. "What is this street made of, that it did not melt into the Sheath?" asked the Twar.

"It is not a street, it is not so wide. It is a crossbar between verticals."

"It is easy to stand on."

It was indeed pocked and rough. They continued, sometimes on the Sheath, sliding towards other verticals and grasping them, sometimes on crossbars they could step or climb onto.

"It seems without end," said Twel grimly, looking ahead and around him. The reddish towers reflected into the black Sheath surface so it seemed to him they were walking giddily at a great height, and below them shone the watery stars.

"There is no way down, and no way in," he said. They sat down on a girder and drank water. "Whatever is here, it is not possible to get at."

"We were to wait for the moon."

"Whatever there is to see, can be seen by starlight."

Twar's hand rubbed at the girder. "There is a break, here, and some markings. Listen."

The Twel concentrated into his Twar's touch. "Perhaps not a break—a letter, part of a letter."

They climbed down, and began to move their hands along the side of the girder, to form some image of letters that were all long as the length of men. It said only the numbers 2, 2, 9, 1.

The Sheath wrapped itself about and against each rising tower as closely as flowing water, but motionless and unbroken—the others with them searched too, but they found no more than some similar numbers on other girders, and nothing on the towers.

They left the city and returned along the rope, but the bodies of their companions remained at Mosc, because they could not bear, in that heat, to burn them. They had touched them, and mourned.

The rope was burnt across at the top of the larger ridge, and after that descent they passed the body of the Goran, and mourned him also, and went more slowly, often crawling. They stopped and rested only till the heat forced them to go on, and some of them were burned, because the rag scraps and their hair burned through, or worse, burned into their feet and palms. But they all lived, twelve pair, and drank water at the camp and slept. They returned to Lenh with the moon's wind, along the ridge swept bare of dust, with the dust heaving past them on both sides, and the air full of it, then slowing as the land rose towards Lenh, long waves of dust foaming up on the earth and running back, and receding.

As they neared Lenh, they spoke to each other, gently, readying for what they had to tell. Twar said to his brother, "Beyond all this death—it is a small thing, but we have also lost time, we should have been gone."

Twel said, "We had to know there was nothing. They had to agree to this in Manj'u. This is a tragedy, yet it might have been something urgent, good and necessary to us."

"Whatever is there, the Sheath will keep and we have to do without," answered Twar. Then he added, "We lived, my brother."

Twel felt the swordbone of their breast plunge and ease at the words, and they breathed deeper, not knowing which of them had been forgiven.

23

The Say leaned back against the rugs, their black hair making one large crown around their black-browed, ruddy faces, that were so alike in look and smile that they were like one mirrored.

"So you are looking for Tasman of Lofot?" said one of them, and it was as if the lips of the other also moved and gave the same smile.

"There was word of her in Lofot lately," said Semer, looking down at his hands.

"The mood changed when the moon greened," said the Say.

He glanced up. "Letters from the east were written into Lofot Book. When the clouds went off the moon, already then, people were rejoicing."

"Did you read those letters?"

"Some read and learned them. We heard and learned them. We left for Uppsal during the time between the floods."

There was a silence.

"You know that the Sorud lived here with Tasman, when they came from Lofot?" Their eyes narrowed.

"I was directed to this house, and told to speak with you."

The Say rose. "Twar Sorud used to work below these rooms. There, you can read what is recently written into Book about the moon. But more than you have learned about Tasman is not written, or whether it is indeed she, or even her name."

"We read badly," said Semer, also standing. "If you know where she is, tell me, because I want to go to her."

"She is at Lenh, unless they have already started east."

"If they are not gone, they will not go till next Darkening. We will travel to Lenh with others who intend to go there."

"She was short-bonded to the Sorud," said the Say. Their look openly sharpened, as if they expected to share a response.

"We know this," answered Semer evenly. "We were told in the city. We also know she is house-bonded to them and they have two—sons. Her mothers told us this. They lived—under the dikes." He straightened a little awkwardly. "The Sorud, I believed, saved her life. They understood quickly what it has taken the world longer to understand—"

"That even the birthfaulted can be valuable—" finished the Say, a little teasingly. "You, for example, because of your twin, became necessarily more beautiful, and more strong."

145

They put out their two hands, and after a moment's hesitation Semer reached out and took them. Between him and the Say lay a human hair rug with some ancient red hair threaded through the black in a pattern of broken arcs. He looked up and met their mirrored gaze. They were almost old women, but the wiry gray springing up from their foreheads only made their hair more black, and their breasts were large, hard and squared by the tight tunic but almost trembling to be loosened, to spill. He remembered the yearning of his weaning and suddenly the desire to suck at those great breasts melted his caution, his body seemed to sink and then gather itself and, as if they knew, the Say's hands tugged him towards them and together they knelt down. He drew out his knife, and carefully cut the taut cloth vertically between those breasts, and released them, and, as the Say leaned back smiling, he guided his brother's blind mouth against one black nipple and turned to the other one, his hands pulling all the soft flesh closer, then moving eagerly between the spreading thighs.

Semer stayed with the Say until the group he intended to travel with was ready—about ten days—and if the Say wished him to remain longer, they did not speak it. Nor did they speak of Tasman except, after that first time on the rug, to tell him it was hers, and to move with him up to their pallet.

The Semer had never been with women before; he had some fastidiousness because of his twin and though desire came sometimes to their body unaccountably, his brother never seemed to initiate it or be conscious of it. The Twar eyes were dull and the look calm—not unhappy, people had told Twel Semer, and he believed this, because he felt the Twar presence as a companionable quietude. The Twel had complete charge of their body. But his brother, he remembered clearly, had sucked milk from their mothers, though he had never learned to eat food. Their weaning had been postponed and when it came, he was aware of a physical loss and longing he hadn't expected, and that must have come from the Twar.

Now at the Say's breasts he saw that the Twar sucked as if his mouth had never forgotten, and when they entered the Say, the Twar was still trying to cling to the breast, and sometimes succeeded. The Say, however, spoke only to the Twel, caressed and kissed at first only his face, though he noticed they had nothing against the Twar mouth on their breasts or on the slack lips of their vagina and their large, loose clitoris. Gradually they forgot to discriminate, however, and lovemaking became more symmetrical, if less intriguing. Twel Semer's desire for their breasts did not diminish either, and when they drooped across him, their weight pulling and flopping at his face and the nipples lingering in his mouth or dragged tauntingly from the corners of his lips, when he felt that dense softness descend on him, as if to erase him, he sometimes cried out and climaxed before their vagina could cover him with its full-lipped mouth.

Semer had two gifts with him—from Lofot, a fragment of true book, and he would bring this to Tasman—as a present, a reconciliation. He had not forgotten the schoolroom in Medical Book, and the little face with its single thick black line of eyebrows contracting over intelligent slate-black eyes—Tasman, whom he had been so furious with, when she told him the truth about his Twar. Everyone else pretended and expected him to pretend—his mothers, his fathers, his teachers, even the other children. They had to—perhaps he himself had made this clear, with his violent protectiveness. He even used to stuff food into his Twar's mouth, he remembered now—and thought up all sorts of complex ways of pretending the Twar could also use their body—he'd even developed a limp, the Twar leg dragging, the Twar arm slowed in movements he imagined as more in keeping with his brother's dormancy.

Twel Semer, reclining on the human hair rug while the Say were out for a time, recollected how he had even tried, when he'd been a bit older, cutting the Twar's cheek to see whether his twin would respond. And the facial muscles did pull into a wince, but it was like the wince of a leaf when you put a flame close to it—and then Twel had been filled with remorse, and caressed his brother's dull face, and kissed him—but Tasman had not only seen through it, she had said it. That, he had been unable to forgive.

He remembered too how the Fa kept taking Tasman in to visit the Kistat—that horrible room. Before Tasman came to Book, they'd tried it with him, too, and he'd gone once, because he didn't know what he was about to see—and he'd seen that—bald, dead twin head, so much more awful than his dear, breathing Twar, as different as death is to life—utterly, not in degree, but in kind—and he had thrown himself into a frenzy of a tantrum and the Fa had never, again, tried to befriend him to the Kistat. But Tasman went on going in, and he remembered the last time, when she, too, had yelled, and ran out—the Kistat died later, soon after Tasman went away, and the Fa and the other teachers said nothing, just closed the door; but the children knew, the twins Vivi, in the wheeled chair, snuck in and came back and whispered it.

He remembered how Tasman was not at Book any more then, how the Fa would not tell the children why, then later said she was going to World. The Semer stayed on till they were weaned, at twelve years old, and then some teachers took them and a few other weaned ones who had been at that Book, out to World, to the dikes and the beaches. Twel Semer still defended and invented his twin, but one night, crouching beside the remains of a fire, and staring out across the water—was it the night of the same day he had cut his Twar and seen him wince like a leaf?—he thought he could hear Tasman's clear voice saying "You are doing that *with both hands.*"

And he'd let go. It was a kind of act, that decision not to act any more, and through it, whitetoothed though they still were, Semer had walked into manhood, and a way of being real in the real world. He remembered how the lights, when he looked back over the dike, were more orange than he had ever seen, orange as blood, the black of the dike more black, the grass spikes along the verges sharper, more clear and so detailed and various he stared for a long time at them in the sheer joy of seeing. The fire's embers popped and sizzled, and the wash of the receding tide was an audible caress. He pulled off the tunic and walked down into the water. He had always swum clumsily, as if to be perfect in his body was a betrayal. Now he let his feet step off the steep shelf and moved in his own harmony. He pinched the Twar's nose shut and covered his mouth, and rolled down into blackness, straightened himself, broke the surface with bursting lungs. As he walked up the dike and home, he felt the simple pleasure of his feet striking the earth—the steady rhythm. And he looked forward.

Home was not so simple. Semer Twel began to spend more time at the market, heard tales, became restless. He had received his body—but to what purpose? People shied off. He had no friends but the old ones from Book, and he felt grown away from them— like his parents, they wanted the old constellation, the pretence of ordinariness. One morning in Darkening at the market, after he had risen to leave with the others, older twins he did not know pushed against him and one said, "Your twin's asleep, we'll help you wake him up," and began slapping the Twar across the cheek.

The old protective fury rose in Semer Twel, and he knocked the twins back against a wall and then down on the ground, but they rolled over and ran off. "Moonfall," said someone in the crowd.

He was still full of anger and had nothing to hit out against. He spat, walked out on the dikes. He decided to be a Traveller and snake hunter.

Semer Twel was not a good Teller. With one mind and no brother to remind him, he forgot the minutiae of his errands. There were, at that time, others to carry word. For a while he spent his time taking younger, weaned twins from the little Book out on the beaches. There was something wrong with all of them. With Semer too, and he was neither student nor teacher. Once he met the Fa in Lofot. He told them he was hunting snake in the Savannas. Having said this, he felt ready to act on it, gathered what he needed and went south in the cars.

24

Tasman clung to the Sorud, and the memory of their other homecomings returned, always they came back with the news bad—Twar blinded, and from the other journeys no improvement in it, or she herself meeting them to tell of the death of babies. Now, though her babies lived, students and friends did not. The Avskel clambered, especially Atwar, demanding the reason for the Goran's death, because they had loved them.

"Why did they die, and you not?"

Twel Sorud explained patiently.

"There was not enough water. We came very quickly and returned quickly because of them, but for them it was a slow journey. The surface of the Sheath is too smooth, even where it is level it is difficult to stand erect, or walk, and when it goes even slightly up, it is impossible without a rope or wind."

"If they had purchase, why did they not climb along the rope?"

"It was not a climb, such a slow slope—I think the rope was too hot and their hands already burnt."

"Or the others began to slide back?" asked Atwar fervently. "So the others released the Goran, so they could save themselves."

"Water, they slid back to them, the last they had." Betwar was kinder.

"Perhaps it was the Goran who released the others," put in Twar.

"They lay down and went to sleep," said Twel quietly. And whispered to himself, "No one woke them. They melted against the Sheath when the sun rose."

They told the boys about the city and Tasman listened, sick at heart. "Did you not leave a sign, that you had been there?"

"Nothing, and nothing will last. The students' bodies, the rope will be burned away. We took back their knives. Their bones will be there a shorter while, and blown by those strong winds. But no one will go to Mosc again. It will be written into Book: that place, if it has knowledge, will keep it hidden forever."

Tasman imagined the white bones of the students, moving and sounding like the sound of Tellers' wrists accompanying their tales in the market, blown lightly and clicking against the silent towers, white on the shiny black surface of the Sheath, sliding and blowing.

"Twar, Twel, it is time to go east. We are a moving city, and cannot stay, until we reach that Book at Manj'u. Let us go now in this Kaamos, and turn north when the heat returns, and not wait any longer."

Twar felt her thin body straighten under his arm. "Are you strong?"

"To move a city? Yes!" (the emphatic) "And we will not be travelling in a wilderness. The cities we pass through will provide for us, and care for us."

"And come with us also," said Twar. "We have seen that already, that it is a new time, a time for the moving of cities."

So they left Lenh, and travelled in a great throng, walking north of the tidal deserts, the season being still dark and the days short with a low sun. In the cities they were met with jubilation and great curiosity, and the Sorud and their family brought always to the coolest house. Tasman stretched out on a mat watching women touch her babies' limbs and wipe them with cool cloths and speak low and wonderingly. She heard the voices of people outside the house singing:

> *"her face is his face.*
> *her voice is his voice.*
> *he will not harm you.*
> *she repeats, she repeats this."*

More people joined them, and the throng increased, but some turned back.

They walked under the moon, which was now free of cloud. The blue of the two great Seas and the lesser ones, and of the great Canal, was deep and pure and beginning to be varied, that is, in some places cobalt, and in others almost turquoise. There was a strange symmetry to the moon's face now, as if a large letter had been written across it, it looked less like a scared, regretful stare, more like a creamy, mottled shield-dish with a great crest on it, a sign in melted sand, but the meaning of the sign was not known.

The Sorud continued in that forgiveness that had come after the tragedy of Mosc. The journey, the real journey in the one direction, was finally under way, and there would be no turnings aside now, they believed. Yet, each time they lay down to sleep, Twel sighed, and Twar at last spoke of their regret:

"We said goodbye at Lenh, but we did not finish with it. It is not good to set forth and leave the past unfinished."

"It is finished as well as we could finish it," said his brother. "I know there is nothing more at Uppsal and Lenh—the wisdom of Uppsal declined before those times, and Lenh we have finished with—what little there was."

"Something is missing."

"It is under the Sheath at Mosc, then. We are like the Fiada in the tale, whose children disappeared in the Savannas—"

Tasman, listening, turned over and leaned across them, her eyes narrowed in concentration. Betwar and Atwar at their fathers' feet crept closer. She began the tale:

> "The Fiada waited in the late day,
> in Lightening, in the old house,
> desert lay to the south,
> their children did not come in,
> they searched, they did not sleep.
> There was no trace in the grass,
> no one came telling.
>
> "Fiada, you must finish with this,
> you must say goodbye to your children.
> The Fiada minds have opened towards the south,
> they opened under the light
> and the light chose a little death
> insignificant, a death of thirst in a tired valley.
> In the city and in the house,
> the Fiada spoke the words of finishing
> and their minds touched the valley and its stems
> and the body of their sons.
>
> "But there was no such valley in the world.
> Fiada, Fiada, you must finish with this,

you must say goodbye to your children.
So their minds opened to the west,
they opened under the light, and the light chose
a brilliant death, a shore death drowning
and the body of the children rolling and wandering.
In the city, in the house,
the Fiada spoke the words of finishing,
and their minds touched the water
and the body of their sons.

"But there was so much coast in the world.
Fiada, Fiada..."

Tasman's voice, soft in the dark house, went on, monotonous, as if perhaps she herself was not listening anymore. It told of the many deaths the Fiada had invented for their children, snake and quicksand, murder and sunstroke and seizure and fever, and how they mourned and could never complete it, because there was no correspondence between their minds and the world. The tale drew to a close.

"Fiada, now you are dying,
you will not outlive your quest, or find rest
in this life, and every day you increase your neces-
sity.
The world is turning from you now
speechless as it was,
gather your minds
close in, to the tiny point,
the smallest place, the going out.
Door, star, tip of the flame,
here is the place they left from, Fiada,
the exact way they went through."

25

S emer came into Lenh as the days lightened imperceptibly, and he found Tasman gone. The trip had been frustration, he was the only Traveller in charge of an exodus of many people, of old people also, who could not walk quickly, and of children. They lost the way once, missing a well, and after that Semer almost went without sleep, going forward in daylight with twins he trusted while the others slept, making certain of the way. They moved in darkness, a slow plaintive crowd of twenty-three pair, and he had to answer many questions at random, and calm many who were fearful. Behind most of them was the flood, and the second flood he had not experienced; they were of the coast and of the higher land and had lived. The only others, a family and two pair of young twins from Uppsal, travelled in the real hope of going on east with Tasman, as he did, and he wondered about the goal of the others, the homeless, who seemed to walk more for the sake of walking than for any real reason. "Why go to Lenh?"

"We heard that Tasman is there, that it is a great city."

"But it is hot there, close to the Sheath."

"We can endure heat. And we can go on from Lenh, north, north and east."

One pair, young women with outlandish, mud-braided hair almost as light as the Semer's, had travelled from Whalsay. "The coast is changed, the plains are under water. It is a great, glistening surface to the west of the high land. It flooded, and then went back. Then the second flood came with the moon's wind."

"How did you come across?"

"Where we lived the ground is uneven. We swam and waded. What was worst was, there were very strong streams, like rivers inside the larger water. But we were not far from the hills, and in that place, Froan, some survived, the ones who went uphill after the first flood. But that was very few, because we believed it was over. The ones on the roofs had gone down into their houses."

Their faces were clean of emotion, now, they spoke simply. They volunteered nothing more.

Semer went down into Book at Lenh, after discharging his flock to people who could feed and house them. There he spoke with old twin women and twin men who sat quietly at screens. The huge place was otherwise darkened and empty.

"They have gone, as you see, and we remain to care for Book, to read and speak what is in Book and what may appear."

"We are lame," added the Twar of the men. "Or we would have gone with them."

Semer sat down, and said, "I want to go with them, and I hope I can catch up with them. I have a gift for Tasman, a piece of true book, but I cannot read it and I do not know what it means."

He pulled down his Twar sleeve and undid the handhair binding on his upper arm, and took out the small metal box. The old women leaned forward, and took it from him, and examined it carefully.

"Where did you find this?"

"In a well wall, in the Savannas, before last Lightening. South of Lofot terminal, about four days' walk, almost directly southwest of Uppsal."

"You have opened it."

"We were unaware of its contents," said Semer hurriedly. "Forgive-us."

They turned the box carefully between their fingers, handing it back and forth from Twel to Twar, holding it close to their eyes. It was dirty with old rust, dented, dark—new, bright scratches showed where he had pried it apart.

"We do not touch or read true book," said the old Twel woman finally. "We will close this away and preserve it for the Sorud Twel." And they handed it across to the old men.

Semer stood up. He took a deep breath, and said quietly, "The Sorud will not return in this generation. The city of history is not in Book any longer, it is moving toward the east. It is not Uppsal, it is not Lenh. True book is the property of the Sorud and of Tasman, and not of the Book of Lenh."

There was a short silence.

"We are not authorized to read it, or to handle it. And you are nothing. You have run with it, not leaving it at Uppsal or the nearest city. If you came to open this container, not knowing of its contents, you are forgiven."

"You are telling us the instructions that Sorud Twar gave you when he used to come here. They are changed now."

"Nothing is changed, we have been given no new authorization."

They sniffed and turned away, and the old men, glancing warily at him, stood up and started limping down the long hallway with its open shelves and doors. They looked back once and their Twar called to him loudly: "If you have read it, tell it to them!"

"When I cannot read the meaning, how could I have remembered it?" called Semer, and made to follow them, but the old women's hands closed suddenly on his tunic, fiercely, so that when he tried to undo the fingers, they were immovable, as if in seizure, the curved black nails hooked into the tough cloth. It was quickest to pull out his knife and cut the cloth away, and then he ran, their feet, shortstepped, slapping after him, the whole place echoing.

He could see where the old men had turned aside between high-piled shelves, and he caught up with them as they were about to push the box into a wall-window, black, its direction downward.

Perhaps, wiser than the women, they had slowed down, delayed their action appropriately. He was able to snatch it from them. He put it between his teeth, the metal scraping with a bad taste, and ran, colliding with the old women who had run up to bar his way, grappling with them. Again their hands clutched into his clothing but this time he yanked off the tunic and left it with them, and ran naked out of Book, up into the bright streets, the billowy dust with its million shards shining in the sunlight. The Semer's braid had come loose. Later there would be a song of praise, not quite serious, about how Semer defeated the ancient keepers of the Book at Lenh, and ran crazed on the burning earth of daylight, with "the hair of two sunflowers" fanned out over his naked body, and true book between his teeth and a knife in his hand.

En natt drömde jag om öknen / sand....

Actually, he could still remember some of the text, some of the sounds he'd spelled out that late dawn, sitting on a turf of grass beside the newly opened well with his feet hanging down into the cool air over the water. Trained in a desultory way to tell letters, he had fixed them, a few of the sounds, into his brain's clutter, by saying them aloud. And it contained the ordinary word *sand*, and the words *glas*, *lins*, *fokus*, which were almost the same as the words in modern speech, and must have meant the same.

Semer was in a hurry, and left Lenh without speaking to the people he had brought with him— some of whom had certainly intended to continue with him, he knew. He ducked into the house where he had been received, where the family were sleeping out the heat—they looked up surprised—

"We are going north," he said, stooping over his things. "We are taking water and food from you in gratitude. We are going quickly without formal leavetaking, in order to catch up with the Sorud and Tasman and their people."

"You are, however, naked—take our tunic—" said the Twar of the fathers, and laughed.

"No, we have what we need to cover our shoulders from the heat—" Semer meant their hair—"and this will do for the rest." And he unrolled the parcel he had carried from Uppsal and wound it around his body, tucking the corners tightly under his armpits. He bound food and water to his thighs and, with the long light handhair, his knife and the box to his upper arms.

When he had got clear of the terminus, and well out on the hot, lonely path, he sat down and opened the box, and, after drinking water and washing his brother's mouth and eyes, he committed the text to memory so that he need not damage it further by touching it again.

Jag vet när fokus kommer—it was almost a meaning, and the Sorud Twel, expert in the old speech, would understand it immediately—and Tasman—he imagined her voice as it had spoken when she was small, clear and righteous (for she had loved righteousness, had her idea of it even then, as he had not) —her voice saying these ancient words and knowing what they meant.

If I can remember it without errors, I will tell it to her aloud, he thought. He stood up. The sun had set, and coolness ran out of the east with the dark. He suddenly felt sick, and almost staggered, as if his body were afraid, and then a tremor ran through the earth, as if his feet, without moving, had slipped under him and caught hold again. *"When fools fall,"* he told himself, *"they believe the world tripped them."* Almost immediately the moon rose, and his shadow sloped west of him, black on brightness. The moon's wind passed him like a long shout, rising in pitch—he braced himself—a small branch struck his legs as if it had been thrown at him and he kicked out at it, and half stumbled. The air became calm. He went on as fast as he could, watching his shadow poured ahead of him north and then northeastward through the brilliant grasses. The moonlight silvered the heavy locks of the Semer hair. He did not look up at the moon.

26

T hey had reached Ust, where there was a lake in marshland, and beyond it a path like a street going north, and a smaller path, a trace through reeds and sandbanks, towards the east. The Travellers from the east had come by this path, Twel Sorud was told, and a large group of people out of Novaya Zemlya would join them here.

Atwar and Betwar had a game of counting: well before night they went ahead, and waiting by the route, and counted the people's passing, then ran to catch up with their parents and tell of it. Always the numbers increased; and to dig wells would be necessary later—*more people, more farms*—this was a city moving, yet still there were tales at daybreak. Babies were born in the marsh lake the day they stayed over, and Tasman, wading nearby with her little ones, lowered them into the dull water on her arms and watched them swim, and cough, and stare, their still somewhat skinny limbs wavering and reaching. Their brothers splashed up, and laughed at them and held them, the downy bodies glistening. The first Liv had a birthmark: the long down on her left upper arm was in one place silvery white, and the boys said they could tell the twins apart because of it. But this twin was also a little stouter, and Tasman recognized them, as she did her sturdy sons, without reasons. She left them playing, and waded back to the Sorud, who were sprawled on the bank where the reeds had been flattened by the coming and going of many people.

Twar said, "When the people come from Novaya Zemlya, we will be a multitude. Is it necessary to travel the same ground within the same night? If we set out this evening, and allow them to follow. Students could remain."

"I must receive them, however. They expect us, the sight of us," said his brother.

"Then send on the people. We will need wells soon. Let it be like the camps towards Mosc, so that everything is prepared, as for an expedition."

"I know I have the power to say, we will travel in this fashion, or in that fashion, the groups also have some harmony within themselves, so far it has been well enough."

"Except that we are pressed." Twar lifted his arm and pushed his hair away from his face. Even though he was sightless, he winced at the light. "I dislike this —pressure—this feel of too many people. Sometimes they move between us and Tasman—"

"If we are to travel with her, we have to accommodate this. She is the ascendant."

"But it is your word. And she dislikes it—my Tasman, can you remember how we walked in the desert?" He took her hand, that she had laid on their breast, and turned towards her with his strange, milky gaze. She kissed his eyes.

"We are walking in the desert again, and between us it is always as it was," she aid gently. "I think in Manj'u they will heal you, Twar."

He turned away into his brother's shadow and closed his eyes. "Sometimes I dream—brilliant dreams. Yet I know, the world is even more brilliant. And I dream of darkness, of shadows—can you believe, I miss the shadowy darkness? There is, in this blindness, too much light."

So the city moved eastward, and grew more populous, and at the beginning of the second month into Lightening, the Avskel counted six thousand, which was the greatest gathering of people ever known. Sorud Twel could not have spoken to them all at once, except with great difficulty from a tree or a hill, and the city was no longer a mass, but a thread, with students and Travellers in the lead, and some wild children, often including the Avskel; and Tasman and the Sorud walked inside a kind of ravelling knot of density near the lead, and the rest farther back, in groups according to their home cities or their speech. But when the moon waxed, there were those who stayed still to look at it, and these fell farther behind.

It was one of these groups that the Semer saw ahead of him, finally, by the marsh lake, with the half-moon hanging almost overhead, and their faces raised to it stupidly.

He walked up and threw himself down beside them.

"Is that water to drink?"

"No, but here is water." It was offered by twins who did not even take their eyes from the moon's face to look at him. Someone had been speaking, near the centre of the group. Behind their heads the marsh lake ran in a wash of moonlight. The speaker's voice continued:

"My eyes are clear now, and I see along the terminator the edge of a great cliff, an abyss, and at its foot the forest. Since the last halfmoon, the forest has risen, and walked. The ochre plains farther into Imbrium have decreased in circumference, and some have disappeared. In the centre of The Sea of Quiet, something will appear as the Terminator passes. This will be soon, watch for it."

People shifted a little, and children were quieted and held up and told to be ready, because of the extreme sharpness of their vision. Semer stared with the others into the massy blue of the Sea, where the terminator shadow crept back with no perceptible change to reveal, suddenly, a glint there, and some children called out, and it looked, from the way the shadow slid out of it, like a transparent disc or bowl, or as if the trees had been pressed down there in the form of an amphitheatre, but the shining was as if its edge was burnt sand, or glass. Semer's eyes teared suddenly and the moon blurred out of his focus. Children were calling out—"a round, deep place in the trees—the trees are flattened down like reeds—no, it is not trees there, a blue plain, smooth—something is on top of it, like water—like thin water."

Now the Terminator had passed and the blue looked solid, unvaried.

Semer asked after Tasman as soon as the group rose and started gathering their bundles. All was confusion. "She is ahead of us, walking with the Sorud." But where was ahead? He walked around to the far side of the group and saw the trampled reeds, and stepped away into them—wherever they were trodden down, he could follow. Twin girls about six years old tagged along, then ran ahead of him: "It's this way —it's this way."

"Wait for the others," he said and when they kept following him, he squatted down and tried to turn them back with his hands. They accepted this as the

beginning of stroking, and looked at the Semer curi-
ously. Their faces were wide like southern peoples',
but their eyes were shallower, and they were swart.

"What is the matter with your twin?"

"He is asleep. He dreams a great deal."

"What does he dream?"

"Ah— can you see your people? Back there—go
back to them. We are going on to catch up with Tasman."

"We are, too, we'll go with you."

"No, we are going to run."

"Carry-us with you!" They clung to him. Finally,
exasperated, he picked them up and carried them
back to the group. He put them firmly down on their
own two sturdy feet, and made a run for it.

It was like moving in and out of small cities with
almost no spaces between them. The closer he came to
Tasman, the more dense was the trail. And it was not
quite clean, and some hastily dug wells were soiled
and empty, and people were hungry and restless and
asking about the next farms.

"Go up ahead, and ask—" and then the press was
thicker. Semer found it faster going on the edges,
where he pushed through reeds and later tree stems
and undergrowth. After two nights of this, he decided
to walk all day instead, and when the group he had
come up with lay down to sleep, he went forward
alone. He slept sometimes, rolling out the wrap he
walked in and lying down on it naked: his body was
now the darkest it could become, a sallow copper
flecked with brown, and did not burn, and the hair
protected his shoulders. Then he got up, and walked
again, and in this way, going around a large group by
climbing a ridge to the north of the path, he passed the
Sorud and their sleeping family in daylight, and did

not see them, and by the next morning had outwalked that group and reached the front of the city. He saw the scouting children, dragging their feet into dawn, and falling asleep almost as they lay down, on the path trace. The Semer lay down apart from them, exhausted from the pace and lack of sleep, and here was pointed out to the Sorud by the children scouts, who had not dared to waken such strange twins, whose body was thrown down naked on its back on a filthy rug of human hair, and whose own hair, yellow as straw, spilled out like straw across their faces.

Tasman recognized them instantly.

Semer Twel opened his eyes into her intent gaze, not knowing where he was, only gradually aware that he was surrounded by people—he sat up, and pulled the human hair rug around his chest to cover himself, and pushed the wild hair back. He saw the Sorud, behind Tasman, and knew them by their authority, and that the one was blind, as he had been told. The other, the Twel, looked stern and old. Semer's hand went to his other arm, the gift.

"Tasman—"

"Semer, I know you, I think—"

He grinned suddenly, amazed. "And I know you." He was looking for what he remembered, trying to make a connection that held. How small she was! He saw her narrow Lofot face in its coif of down, as if its edges were blurred, while the features in the centre, under that thick, horizontal brow-line, came into sharpest focus: eyes narrowset and serious, the sclera glinting, small nose that had a flat bridge and then immediately flared, over a full mouth with small lines that trembled at the corners as if her smile was seldom and the muscles unused and uncertain, and at the eyes' outer edges, tiny lines. The righteousness was still there, in the even gaze, and it was as then, almost prohibitive, yet suited her in her maturity. And space. For even though he now realized he had thought of her almost constantly, he was not used to her, the way her family was, to that sleeve of white space her head rose into in its singleness and singularity. No wonder people were calling the moon her housebond now, in the songs.

He stood up, and saw a baby's head and fists emerging from its bundle strapped to her side, and another one, separate, tied at the back of her waist in a kind of sash. In his confusion he took them to be the Avskel, the sons he had heard of. He stood up. "We have a gift for you," he said, stammering slightly.

"Yes," said the Sorud Twel in a calm voice. "It is wrapped around your body."

"Ah—the rug also—it is yours, Tasman, the Say told us, and so we brought it to you—and in Lenh we were forced to leave our shirt—" Semer looked down, and struck at the rug and pulled out a couple of green stalks, and would have gone on with this futile task if they had not stopped him.

"Sit down with us."

They went forward a little and sat down, the Twel's look making clear, to the other adults, at least, that they needed a space of privacy, though several children drew close again, and squatted around them. The Avskel were not there, then, though they came up later, breathless and staring, and pushed in under the Sorud arms.

Tasman unstrapped the babies and laid them across her knees. Morning had broken, a broad daylight spread across the clearing and warmed with detail all the people around them. They could hear the sound of stone against stone up ahead—the beginning of a new well—and one of the Liv whimpered and Tasman without looking down rolled it a little on her thigh with the flat of her hand.

Semer had unwound the arm pocket, and removed the box, which he stretched out to her in his open hand. "This is the gift. We ran with it from the Savannas, but we ask you to *forgive-us*. It is in a speech we cannot read, and it was my decision that the Book it belongs to is with the Sorud Twel in the moving city."

Tasman looked into his eyes then and smiled. Turning the box over, she said to the Twar, "This gift is a box of metal, Twar, as small as my two palms." She placed it in his hand.

"It has been in the earth."

"We found it in an old well we reopened, in the Savannas west of Uppsal. It was in the wall, which looked like the wall of a ruin—like the walls below the Say house—and there was perhaps more, but we could not find anything else immediately, so we marked the place. It is near a city named Vajkas."

Sorud Twel opened the box.

"It is true book," Semer went on eagerly, "and I have learned the words, but I cannot tell what they mean." He remembered suddenly that he had wanted to repeat them to Tasman, but now that they were no longer in his hands, it seemed as if they were not in his mouth either.

The Twel was so still that the group held their breaths. Only the ring of stone on stone, and the shuddery sigh of one of the babies, broke the silence. The sun rose, its hot red light patchy across the people's faces and their dark, dirty limbs and garments.

The Twel had not disturbed the leaf in its bed of fragments, except to slide the bits that covered it off its edges with one careful finger. Now he read it, aloud, in the old speech as it was written.

En natt drömde jag om öknen
sand, brännande sol
Jag vet när fokus kommer

Jag är bara en delvis
levande människa

I sanden ligger halvt begravd
en stor lins, av
skört glas, repor
från sanden och vinden

Korrelatet, motstycket
är det omöjliga   Det är
nödvändigt att vi inte vet
exakt vad vi gör, exakt var vi står

Then he closed the box and looked up. "Tasman, will you carry this, or shall we?"

"You, certainly, when I have learned it."

Twar laughed. "Is it not learned already?"

"The sounds—but I am not sure of some of the words. *Repor*—Twel, is it what you were looking for at Mosc?"

"I'm not sure. It is only a bit of leaf, a dream. Yet it has followed us, as if it had meaning, and it seems to me to be complete, if I could understand it. As if something we had lost or left behind us came hurrying after us, to complete us—" he smiled a little, his face still looking inward, and softening. "I did not think there was wisdom west of Uppsal."

The Avskel, exhausted, had rolled into sleep, and Tasman lay down by the Sorud, suckling her babies, while the Sorud, supported on their elbows, spoke with her softly. Semer knelt nearby—he had a sense of being in attendance, expectant that they would ask him some important questions—gradually he realized that there was nothing of importance he could add, and that he had been forgotten. He pulled up his knees to his chest, and went back to extracting bits of dirt and straw from the human hair rug, glancing up at them from time to time. Their backs were to him. Tasman's feet, crossed at the ankles, were nearest. He saw how the black down stopped over the footsoles, that were thick, high-arched, dirty, and covered with old scars, and one new scar with a tender pink edge. Cautiously he shifted the rug a little, and eased it under her feet in the soft sandy earth. She kicked out as if a grass blade had disturbed her, and recrossed her feet, and he saw with satisfaction that the rug was well under them. He was hungry, but he had slept, so he went off to ask for food, and ate, and washed his mouth and his brother's, and returned. They lay as they had lain, except Tasman had rolled over on her back, asleep, with her hair shading her babies and one arm across her face. Her other arm was stretched under the Sorud shoulders, and Twar Sorud slept, his cheek on her arm, but the Twel had the box open again, in the shadow of their body, and was gazing into it. Semer sat down, but could not get his attention, and after a time he went over to some young men who were awake, and told them everything that had happened to him.

27

I t was, however, Tasman who prepared a new tunic
for the Semer, and she pulled it on over their heads
and helped drag out the locks of their hair, as if they
were children. And Semer was made to belong, eating
with them and sleeping beside them—though he
mostly walked forward with the Avskel and the half-
wild children. To the boys he told those things he
would have liked to have told Tasman, about growing up, and a great deal about hunting snake—and
these accounts were perhaps made a little more glori-
ous, certainly when Atwar retold them among his
companions.

"Fadar, the Semer have killed two snakes, and
from their skins received a house, but it is under
water in Lofot now."

"And they go naked."

"Semer Twel says it does not matter, and if we
meet snakes on our journey, he will kill them for us."

"That is good, Atwar."

"You have seen a snake, Fa, but the Semer have
killed two."

Twar pulled his son close to him. He missed the
body of Atwar, the time when the boy, unweaned and
weaned, had kept close and told him many things—

yet it had been a time of anger and silence. The earlier times, when the Sorud, alone, had gone out into the night Savannas, he did not miss—then, he had thought he was happy, yet he had been without Tasman and without children. Betwar and Atwar had not existed, nor had the baby girls, and even the ordinary marvelous use of his eyes belonged to a time before his children. He smelled the boy's hot, squirming body, childsweat had a sweet, smoky smell—these were his two little wild ones, his little snakes....

Gradually he spoke more with Semer, and found in him some of his own youth's daring, but Semer had no twin to temper him. Tasman had described the Semer twin to Twar—"He has a dreamy, inward look, as if he were wise, but Semer says he cannot think, he is about as a tree, that consciousness." But Semer had said, "It is not the worst thing, to keep a tree," and Tasman almost envied him.

"You are changed," she had said then, giving Semer a direct look, and he would have answered her in a rush of words, but the Avskel ran against him, making some demands, and that conversation was broken off.

> *One night I dreamed of desert*
> *sand, burning sun*
> *I know when the focus comes*

"Will come" Twel Sorud corrected himself—"*When the focus will come*. Where is that lens, then, that will focus? Is it that glass told of in the letter from the east, in which the moon's expression is made clear, at Manj'u under the Sheath?

"Deserts can change," he went on, "yet I do not think so. It was written then, but it concerns these times. I have considered this and considered this. I am afraid of this scrap of leaf, because I do not want to believe in a prediction."

"That is the Moonfall heresy you have fought all your life," said Twar.

Twel sighed. "Tasman, what do you think? It would be hard, at our age, to have to fill in the door of our house and open one in another direction—"

"For me, not so hard—remember that the Travellers from the east told us also, of what was to come, and what they told is from the true book they had studied, what is set out there, in what they called First Script. Perhaps the whole world knew of it, and this is another fragment of that knowledge."

"Then where is the focus and who knows of it? Is it possible we are travelling away from it? Is it back in our own country?"

"We are taking this with us, anyway," she answered, "and we have time to think about what it means. Whoever wrote it dreamed of a desert they had never seen, and we are going to cross deserts before Manj'u. That has to be enough."

The babies born in the marshlake could not thrive, and they died about ten days after, and other very young children were sick; it was as if milk would not bind in them, they wasted because it would not stay in their bodies. Their mothers wet their lips with salt (for, of food, they carried salt and yeast and crushed meat of hips). There were women from the Medical Book in Novaya Zemlya, and they knew this sickness but not how to cure it. Some of the babies got better, but the smaller ones weakened gradually, and died, and Tasman's babies died within a day of each other, before they were five months old, even though the one, the Twel, had not seemed so sick, only quiet.

So in the moving city there were no children born in the winter sixmonth of 450 and 451 that lived, and that sixmonth was later called Dearth.

When they mourned aloud, they stripped the stems of two trees, the Avskel cutting away the green bark, and Tasman buried, at the foot of each stem a lock of hair from the babies. But she cut the white down from Atliv's arm, so one lock was black, and one white.

They wrapped the bodies of the children in grass and branches, and burnt them up, and ate the ash. But she saved one rib from each child, and wore these from that time on, around her upper arms.

Semer left them to this, though he wept privately, and such was his grief (says the tale), *"that it rose in the Twar's throat as sap rises in the season of Lightening, and out of his eyes ran the first two tears."*

I am only a partly living person
"Or, *partly alive*—such words can refer to me, because my body has only one mind," said Tasman.

"The Outdead would not have referred to you so —you are as they were. Remember this was written by one of the Outdead."

"Yet, Twel, it is prophecy, it tells of these times."

"Who among us is other than partly alive," the Twar burst out passionately, "who have lost our children to death?"

Twel and Tasman talked as they walked forward, and Atwar again clung to the Twar side, but Betwar wanted to be close to his mother and at night he secretly drank the milk that would not cease filling her breasts.

28

S emer walked ahead. What had happened to the
Sorud family distanced him from them, and for a
time the boys did not seek him out. They were moving into inhabited country again, and nearing Pechor,
and the pass over Ura, and to the east they could see
the high mountains. The land was reddish and fertile,
and wherever it was irrigated there were farms. People lived in small cities, the houses spread out, and
greeted them with amazement, and there was enough
food. To the north was a broad lake, and from it water
was directed through canals, and the whole width
and length of that valley.

The Sorud and Tasman were invited into a house,
and it was cool, and they slept long. But towards
evening there was a tremor in the earth, and then a
great crashing of the moon's wind, and they ran up,
and everything was blowing about—peoples' parcels,
mats, branches and roofgrass, and in the irrigated
wood the nearest line of planted trees bent over and
broke off at the root, and afterwards lay along the
ground. Also, a fire some children had made caught
at a roof, and people ran and put it out with their
clothing.

When everything was again quiet, Semer Twel, coming up to the Sorud, told them privately that he had felt this before, but he had believed it was a disfunction in his own body. Then the men of that house told them that, in this valley, the earth had been shaking at times since the beginning of Lightening, and no one knew what caused it, but they believed it was the moon's wind, or what caused that wind, which was, they supposed, the nearness of the moon.

That night they remained at Pechor, and the people sat outdoors among the houses, where the earth was plain and hard and clean. The Sorud went up with some others on to a raised roof, and after the letter from the east had been told, Sorud Twel spoke aloud to all the people there.

"Past these mountains is a new language, and we are waiting for those Travellers who will meet us and show us the way. It is beginning to get hot, and we will go somewhat north, because of the long day. We know that there is desert between these mountains and Manj'u, and we cannot cross it, but will travel around it to the north with people who will advise us. What is important is water."

The earth trembled, and a sigh went through the crowd, and children cried out.

Semer stood up—he was on a roof near the Sorud, and Tasman with him, seated on the rug he had laid out for her (he continued to carry it and it was now his custom to bring it to her).

"Need we wait for these Travellers? Can we not go to meet them? It is getting lighter and hotter every day, and the earth is not stable in this valley."

Sorud Twel turned to the men beside him, Pechor people, whose Twar spoke. "There are two passes, and they will come through the nearer one, at the defile, almost certainly. The main pass is to the north, and easier, when we are so many. If we go now we will miss them."

"Some can go on, some can wait," called a voice.

"Do you know that pass?" called another voice, a woman's.

The Pechor twins got up, and their Twar answered: "There are none here who have gone through it, but at Abez there are. It is not difficult. We have walked to Kosyu. That is an easy path. But without these eastern Travellers to help us on the other side, we could lose our way."

"Are there not always people," said Sorud Twar to him, "who know the land they live in, as you do, and can guide us?"

"Perhaps there is only desert. If there is a city, would we not have heard of it? But we only know of Pur where the Travellers came from, and it is a very great distance further east."

"We are almost sure," added his Twel, "that there is no city close to that pass at its eastern opening. If there is, it looks east, and speaks that language."

"We will wait a few days," said Twel Sorud. "Because Travellers have come twice in this Darkening, and then told you they would come once more. They should have been here by now, and they will certainly arrive soon."

But the days passed, and the world shook. Semer, walking out with the Avskel early one morning, towards the mountains, met people coming from the farms and asked them, "Where is that defile the Travellers will come through?"

They pointed directly east, towards a round peak behind lower ones. It was black against the dawn sky, and below, where the other hills crossed it, filled up with a paler light, like smoke lit from below.

"That is Narod, the greatest mountain. The defile comes from behind it, passing to the north of it from behind it."

"Is it difficult?"

"We have been told that parts of it are difficult. Sometimes, lately, there have been noises from the mountains, heard even here in Pechor, so we think it has become more dangerous." They pointed to a large tree at the edge of the farms, where the ground began to rise. "There is where the Travellers shout to us, when they are coming to Pechor."

Semer returned with the children, and they pressed before him into the house. He crouched inside the door, and Tasman, seeing his look, asked, "What is it, Semer? Are you ready to speak to us?" so that he was released from demanding the Sorud's attention. They were kneeling on the pallet, and turned towards him.

"What do you wish to say?" asked the Twel in an even voice.

"We will go through the defile," said Semer, as authoritatively as he could. "And meet the Travellers. The rest of you can start north immediately, towards the easier pass. And I will tell the Travellers this, and turn back with them, and meet you further on."

Sorud Twel said, "If there is a clear path, then go to meet them. Surely they will be coming through the defile now, and be here before the last people have gone north from Pechor—and in that case you will be able to come back with them, and catch up with us."

"But, if I don't find them on this side of the defile, I will go north along the east side of the mountains, because it seems to me, when they always use this way, it must be by far the quicker one."

"Do not lose yourself from us, Semer," said Twar, and reached out his hand till it touched the rope of coarse hair.

Semer, crouching before them under the low roof, heard the warmth in his voice and closed his own hand over Twar's. He looked from the Twar's blind, ravaged face to the Twel's, gaunt and thoughtful—Semer feared Twel still—and then to Tasman beside them, and general ache of love, as if telling him he ought to make a finishing, constricted his chest. Tasman must have seen it in his look, because she intercepted him quickly: "It is not finished. If you go from us, you are going towards us, to meet us, that is all."

Betwar pulled down the door curtain, and closed it, and they lay down and slept, and Semer stayed and slept close to them, close enough to see how Betwar crept in against Tasman and whispered, "Ma—" and heard her whisper, "You are weaned," and his answer, "But it hurts you, let me, as in the tale."

Semer heard the Twel then, saying in a low voice, "A little then, Betwar, we are part of a tale ourselves, after all—" and slept to the comfortable small sounds of Betwar sucking, and their breathing.

Towards evening he woke, alert, and crawled across to the door and looked out. The valley lay with the late sun-shadows across it, and the long curved thread of the daymoon, cool white, hung overhead, its details pale and grayish. There would be an eclipse soon now. Had the earth rocked, or had he dreamed it? Moonfall—the focus—

His brother coughed, and by habit he put his fingers into the slack mouth and then wiped it with the back of his hand, and with their braid-end. He stepped over the threshold and looked to the east, at the mountains. The light on them was flat now, and they looked flat and impassable, like a great wall. But

there was a path between the farms, and a tree, and
then he would find the way. His brother coughed
again, like a sob, and he glanced at him. His Twar was
facing the moon, and a large tear, translucent, hung
on his almost white eyelashes. Semer Twel touched it,
then tasted its salt on his fingertip. He would find a
cloth with water and wash the gentle face. Sometimes
it seemed it to him his brother's look was almost like
a smile.

29

S emer had walked east all night, and lain down to
sleep in high open hills, and slept, and woken
again, before he knew they had followed him. He
opened his eyes, squinting in the low sunlight, and
rolled over and reached for water—and his hand encountered the hot, living arm of a little boy.

It was Betwar, fast asleep.

Semer jumped up and stared around, and saw
Atwar almost immediately, sitting farther off with his
arms wrapped around his knees, in the shade of a
stone, and watching him.

"Betwar would come, so I had to come," he said.

But when Semer woke Betwar, he also said, and
more convincingly, "Atwar would, so I had to go with
him."

Semer clapped his wrist against his throat in exasperation. "It will be discovered, however, and the Sorud will fetch you back."

"No," said Atwar, his thin, almost black hands pulling at some grass at his feet—"They have already gone north, and we will not be missed for days. They will believe we are with the first people."

Betwar added: "That is because Atwar contrived for us to go forward with them, when they set out in that direction—then we dropped back, and ran behind the farms, till we reached the path you had taken."

He flung himself into Semer's arms. "It is a tale, Twel Semer, do not be angry. If you are angry, it will be told in the tale, that the Semer did not *forgive-us*."

"Forgive-us," repeated Atwar, but Semer, looking angrily at him across the sward, saw absolutely no repentance on his face, or in his stance, for he had sprung up, and his legs were almost dancing with excitement.

Semer stamped away from them, over to the slope he had come up at dawn, and looked down across the long range of broken hills he had crossed. He had not expected to go back without the Travellers to guide him, and he had not marked the way. He pushed at a large, loose stone with his foot, but it sat deeper than he thought, and it took both hands to wrench it loose and send it rolling down the scruffy hill. It bounced, thumped, came to rest in a far hollow. Great red-black clouds hung in the west, in a sky that was nearly green where the sun had left it, and the edges of slope by slope below him, sharpened by the last light, seemed to lose their distance and fold in against themselves flat and vertical, with darkness rising between them, squeezed upward by this flatness, this visual compression. How many hills lay between here and Pechor? And now the city had gone—by the time they could return, gone even to the stragglers, the last ones. He turned back to the children, who were watching him warily.

"Did you give any word to anyone of this?" They were silent.

"Do not any know of it?" He looked at Betwar.

Betwar burst into tears. "Atwar said, our mother will know we are with you, because we are always with you."

Semer groaned. "She will guess it—how can she know it? The Twel—" he shuddered visibly, and felt cold prickles of sweat along his backbone. "Ah—our body is afraid of your Fadel! He will tell me, I ought to have foreseen and prevented this."

"No, Semer, how could you, if he did not? He is our father."

Semer stroked Betwar. "Now, at any rate, you must answer to me. We must go on, because it is too late to go back, and whatever is done will be done because of my decision, not yours."

Betwar's body relaxed then, and Atwar came over to them, and allowed Semer to embrace his also. "We will do as you tell us," he said soberly.

When they had eaten and drunk water, they set off in twilight, the way being mostly level and the barren hills rising on either side, but still open. Atwar's spirits lifted again and he chattered.

"We could not let you go by yourselves, like Travellers, with no others to help you, and in a country where you have never been. We are strong, and we have carried food and water with us, as you see."

"At least you have done that. What other help you can be to us, I do not know. You cannot even divine, you have no talent for it, either of you."

"Can you, Semer?"

"A little. We are not good at it."

They continued into the mountains, but the nights were very dark, and once, having entered a low gully, they reached a place they could not get out of by going forward, and after this happened, Semer began to mark the directions. Two days after, when he was cutting a mark at dawn, he saw that a mark had been cut almost under his, in the stone—an old mark, but scratched again recently, and when he had shown this to the boys, he said, "We know now that we are nearing the defile, and will get across quickly, and go north."

"We are so quick," said Betwar confidently, "that we will stand and greet them at the other pass."

"But where are the Travellers?" asked Atwar, as he had asked many times. "What if we go twel around a stone, and they go twar and miss us? What if they went by when we were in the gully?"

His constant questioning exasperated Semer. "They will find us by the noise of your voice. We will not miss them now."

But that day they slept with their bodies stretched across the level place directly under the marked stone.

Sickness woke him, as if his stomach had turned over. Immediately the earth moved, the boys wakened, and they jumped up, staggering. It was still day but dark, and they saw that the white sun had walked behind the moon, its rays foaming at the limb as it disappeared. Semer stared around at the suddenly day-black mountains. From a distance came a sound like thunder that increased, a long roaring, and then that stopped, and they heard the scratch and thud of one or two stones knocking against a nearby hill as they fell down, and then that stopped, and in the silence they could hear a constant, distant crumbling—a whispering, as of water falling continuously from a great height.

"What is that?" asked Semer sharply.

"Ah—it is what I heard when we came here, it is not a new sound," said Atwar. "No, I heard it also," said his brother.

"Let us go on, and get through this," said Semer, "while the sun walks behind the moon."

They gathered their bundles hastily and went forward through steeper and steeper cliffs, in the darkness of the day.

When the sun's light emerged again, they had reached the source of the sound. They stood at the entrance of a great, round valley, and to their right, broken off close to them so that the valley had a short arm to the south, was a very high, long cliff, that curved in front of them and above them. Narod's peak was now hidden behind it, and at its base were long hills of loose earth and stone, that fanned out into the valley half obliterating a dried-out, ancient streambed that skirted them. The north side of the valley was crammed with great boulders and a shorter cliff, and behind that ridge was a mountain. Ahead of them, the valley narrowed and seemed, from this view, to close. At the re-emergence of the sun, the heat was intense, the contrast of sunlit rockface and dark brown shadow almost hurtful, and Semer pulled their hair over the boys' faces, and over his eyes and his brother's.

The source of the whispering sound was not water, but a rain of dust and earth, and sometimes stones, that fell continuously off the brink of the great cliff overhead. Semer and the Avskel kept outside of it, walking on the dry streambed, moving very slowly because of many great, round stones. But farther in, they could not climb up a short bank of rock, gouged vertically and made slippery by the force of the now dead stream. So they were forced to go in under the cliff's brink and walk across the loose, steep hillside, where every step they took was also a downward slide, so they had to climb to keep level. They would have to cross the earthfall. Semer put himself between the boys and the cliff, and they covered their heads with their sleeves and arms. But when they entered the earthfall it rained on them with the force of a standing wave breaking, almost knocking them down. Semer unrolled the human hair rug and covered them, and so they ran and scrambled with Semer bleeding, till they got across.

The valley closed there, except for a single cleft like a black slit, marked on both sides with letters they could not read, and the boys re-marked it, using the blood on the Semer's legs mixed with spittle and dirt. Semer pulled the boys after him inside the gap, to where it widened a little and was in deep shadow. Here they lay down and slept, because they were exhausted.

And a snake came, but they did not hear it, because of the general noise of that valley.

30

Semer was dreaming of the Travellers, that they appeared over Narod's peak, but their heads were huge, and their faces mauvish and grinning, moving in front of and behind each other on long, supple necks, like the sun sliding behind the moon, and when he could only see one head, he woke, and Atwar was screaming.

The boys were out on the shale, and the snake was on Atwar.

Semer ran and, timing himself, leaped up against the rough curve of the snakes' head as it turned and charged down on him, and he scrabbled and grabbed at the flap of its nostril and hung on, and pierced its eye with his knife, then felt for the other and pierced it also, but he was sliding, and its tail harmed him as it flung itself over, the shale roaring as it thrashed. Then he tried to move and could not, but by chance the snake threw itself back into the hill of shale and went writhing and whipping in that direction, towards the earthfall, silent because it had no voice, its frenzy still inward and not connected to the ones it had hurt, and who had hurt it in turn.

Betwar was inside the cleft, and Semer, staring back, saw that he had somehow pulled his brother in after him: there was a track of blood on the earth. He tried to move, but it felt as if the snake's weight still covered the twel side of his back and pressed him down, and he could not draw breath deep enough to shout. He heard a new roaring of the shale, and saw that the snake had turned around again and reared itself up, its great neck swaying. If it can smell it is smelling us, he thought, if it remembers it is remembering us. He tried again to speak, but only managed to whisper, "Betwar, *help-us*," and found Betwar there, close to him, leaning over and whispering back, "Semer?"

"Help-us."

Now, with the boy's skinny hands pulling at his armpits, he could move, and they got to the cleft and partly into it, Semer striking the earth with his feet and clawing it behind him, like a swimmer.

The body of Atwar was covered with blood and Semer thought that he was dead, but then he heard him whimpering. Betwar pulled Atwar easily further in, so Semer could get inside the cleft, which at its entrance was hardly wider than the girth of men, and then they heard the head of the snake (or the forepart, because it had no head, only a truncated neck with mouth and eyes and flapped nostrils on it) striking against the opening of the cleft again and again, and when he looked back, he could see it against the light; and it seemed, under those dull, maddened blows, that the cliff itself was shuddering.

31

They lay in a pleasant meadow (because on that side of the mountains there was a draught from the north and some small, tough forest, and it sometimes rained), and here the Travellers had made a shelter of stems which Betwar had covered with branches.

Semer recovered so that he could walk about, but his side was a dark bluish mauve and he breathed very shallow and spoke low, so that his body would not be enraged. The Travellers bound splints made of stems around Atwar's legs, and a kind of box of stems from his back down his right thigh, and the breaks in his skin began to heal, slowly. Also, they cut themselves and gave him their blood to drink, mixed with white dust scraped from an escarpment past the trees. He coughed much, and slept or half-slept, and spoke aloud and shouted in his dreams; and either the Semer or Betwar lay always close to him in the shelter, to squeeze water into his mouth and hold and stroke him.

Semer's recollections of the coming of the Travellers were brilliant but confused—their faces black with consternation, leaning over Atwar in the defile, their incomprehensible, fast speech. They had shiny bluish hair pulled tightly back, and broad faces with very smooth, almost hairless skin and shallow eyes, and they were strong. Then their Twar had spoken to Betwar much more slowly, in real speech, and Betwar had gabbled about the snake—and they had looked out of the defile, stepping over Semer, but had not gone out of it into the earthfall valley. They came back quickly, and after turning Semer over and looking at him, concentrated on Atwar, stripping off their long tunic and wrapping him in it and staunching him with cloths. Then they left but returned after a time with a kind of raft of stems, and eased the boy onto it, and carried him away, Betwar following. During this time (it was morning) Semer lifted himself enough to turn and see, through the opening behind him, part of the snake's body across the gap, and he did not think it lived. But the next time he looked, it was gone.

Again the Travellers returned, and gave him water, and walked with him, supporting him, until they came out into the meadow. Their name was Ve.

"On that cliff is written, *A snake was seen in this valley in 442*," said the Ve.

"But we could not read it."

"And if you could, even so, everywhere, a snake has been said to have been seen."

But Semer berated himself that, having killed two, and being called a snake hunter, he had not been prepared for it, and had not killed it.

"It will die of its blindness," said the Ve. But Semer was not finished with this, and when his body forgot, and drew a deep breath, and he felt the dark ache claw down his side, his anger flared in him. He saw, too, that Betwar was afraid, and kept looking back, and he heard him whispering to his brother,

"Hurry and cure yourself, because we need to go north quickly, to our fathers."

But Atwar could not hurry, and when his skin was healed and he could eat and speak, he still could not walk. He was very thin now, and black with his body's rage, but his mind was clear, and his eyes burned, and he talked of nothing but the snake, because he wanted Semer to go back and find it, and kill it.

"It is dead of its blindness," said the Ve, in their slow speech, explaining. But later Semer heard them down on the slope near the trees, talking fast in their own tongue. He could not understand their words, but he suspected, from their glances towards the west, that they intended to go back to the snake and take its skin, if they could find it.

So that evening on a pretense of finding chalk for Atwar, he left them and went in among the bluffs, and cut a straight stem, and stripped it. Sitting under the bluffs, he cut off a lock of his hair and separated it, and braided it tight into a string. Then he bound the stem to his knife blade, and tied it to his arm, and went secretly up into the path under Narod, and into the defile. About midnight he came out by the earthfall, and looked all around him.

A wedge of black shadow hid the cliff's face, and the waning moon was behind it on a bright sky, its great cool rim clearing the brink that went on crumbling away, as it had crumbled away from the beginnings of the world. The noise was like the noise of a snake on shale and like his memory of the place. He walked into the earthfall because there was no other direction, covering himself with his sleeves and scrambling forward. When he emerged, he saw the snake lying almost covered, half in and half out of the moonlight in the last fan of shale, where the cliff curved to the south. Sand and tiny stones clung to its slide, and its scales, as large as mens' footsoles, looked black except where they turned upwards, where each held an upturned crescent of shiny green, reflecting the sky. Some scales were horned, ridged, imperfect. Semer's mind pictured suddenly his first snake, whose belly when he had turned it had been closewoven, sleek, almost white (it was much smaller than this one), the spill of its whitish blood like semen. This one had wormed its way deep into the shale so the loose earth nearly hid it, but he could see it was not dead, because it twitched a little as it lay, and the gravel whispered and it was as good as his already, horrible and valuable.

To kill snakes was not as in the tales, because face to face you could not, and there was seldom any real cunning to it, either. If you found one, and it was at rest, you could perhaps do it. Semer looked at it and laid his plans.

The moon had set and the early light was growing out of the east. He could see through the earthfall the green, blurred, steadily cooling and whitening sky against which the ridge was an undifferentiated wall of darkness, while at its foot a cloud of pallor, the light on the dust from the fall, seemed to rise out of the shale like smoke. He drew his knife, and with a sudden movement kicked at the gravelly, glistening flank. The snake rolled, nearly throwing him down the slope as the shale poured off its side, and one nostril appeared, under an awful, crusted eyepod. He snatched the nostril flap and clung to it, and was hoisted off his feet as the head reared, but he held fast, and drove the knife directly inward through the scabby, black crust of the near eye, till only his fist remained, mucky at the end of the shaft. This time, what life was left in the snake was pierced, and its long tired muscle flexed almost gracefully, and sunk back like a rope in water. Semer, sliding easily to the ground against it, felt its last, weakening tremor like a sigh of silence. He pulled out his knife, and unwound the wet bonds of hairstring from the black shaft and threw them down. A small happiness rose in him as he worked, as if it came out of the huge, solid, dead flank of flesh he leaned against. He could not dig the snake free and take its skin, which would be a long work, but he cut as great a piece as he could, for Tasman, and peeled it back, and two smaller pieces for the boys, and took those parts which were most valuable—the nostril flaps and jaws for tools, and some other parts for oil and bags and medicines. By evening he was finished.

"Now you can stink as you please, and others harvest you," he said aloud. He was covered with sweat and fat and could hardly keep his feet for exhaustion. He leaned for a moment against the hacked flesh. Its stench in the dayheat was nauseating. Then he felt, past all those rank, gouged gifts, the familiar sickness in his gut, and almost immediately the earth shuddered. A huge rain of earth and rock poured off the brink and roared down behind him. When it had subsided, he gathered his prizes, covered himself, and went through the earthfall with his burden.

32

I n the end of Lightening on the long days, Tasman
stood in the threshold of a door that was not hers,
in Muzh, and looked southward impatiently. Muzh
was the seasonal hamlet they had found at the eastern
opening of the pass—it was deserted, with its wells
covered and its doors filled in. And she saw them,
coming forward between the roofs, with the Sorud
who had gone back to meet them. Her son Betwar ran
into her arms, and her son Atwar peered between the
heads of the Semer Twel and Twar, so that it seemed
as if his own hair was yellow, and shouted, "Ma, we
have skins for you!" As the Semer knelt in front of her,
Atwar reached out his emaciated arms, and she
touched him. The others loosened the Semer's hair,
that bound the raft of stems to their back, and lifted
the raft off and carried Atwar inside on it.

Now the women from the Novaya Zemlya Book
looked at him. They took the splints off his legs, and
replaced one, and said that he would walk again, but
he must first wait for that one leg to heal. Semer did
not come in; he flung himself down against the roof
with his legs stretched straight out in front of him in
the dust, and his face bared to the sunlight.

The Ve had reached Muzh first, ahead of them, marking the way and running fast, and the Sorud, hearing what had happened, had left immediately to run to meet Semer and the children, while Tasman waited. There were many hundreds who stood about as they came in, the Semer walking with the raft bound to their back, and Atwar eagerly looking ahead for Tasman.

Semer's fear of the Sorud Twel had pushed his feet forward on that journey, as if he were running from him, not towards him. Whenever it grew too hot, he had lain carefully down, and they slept as they had walked, the bonds of his hair still holding the child, and Betwar gave them food and sometimes found them water. They had gone through the shade of trees, because it was almost continuously light; the draught from the north cooled the air, but every step hurt the Semer's side, as he was forced to breathe deeply, and this angered his body.

Atwar's arms were free, and he pulled the rest of the Semer hair over him like a tent, and chattered. He told Semer that he had seen the snake that day and had gone out, "because I decided to kill it. But I would have called you. It was resting, as I thought, but all at once it lifted itself, and fell on me."

"You have no knife, little Atwar, how could you have killed it?"

"I thought I would look quickly at it, and then call you."

Betwar, trudging along beside them, said, "It was only a moment, Semer. Atwar saw it and woke me and went out to it, and it fell on him, just as quick as I have said this."

Then Semer saw ahead of him the Sorud at an opening in the trees, running forward as he was running, the way tired men run.

"We met the Ve. We have been looking for you."

But the Sorud Twel's look, as Tasman's would be, was for his sons, and only later did he ask Semer certain questions. Most of it he had heard already, from the Ve.

The city moved east as the season moved towards Kaamos in the dark of Darkening, and reached Pur in the cool, short days. They walked through open Savannas and rolling, short-forested land with welcome streams.

The moon's wind was stronger and more savage, so now it was dangerous to be among trees when it passed, and some people were hurt by the thrashing of branches. And the earth shuddered, so often that people began to make names for what it did, they said that it shrugged, or shivered (as in fever), or spoke (if there was noise). Semer knew, now, that his body registered this moving of the earth earlier than the others, because a kind of physical dread, like a fist, would seize their body, and then, certainly, the earth would shake and people would cry out. It felt as if he were going to cast up food, and his Twar's eyes teared at that time; and later this was the way people were warned.

At Pur, they crossed a stream so wide and deep they had to swim as well as wade, and were dispersed far down its eastern bank, where they lit fires that were like a long city. Tasman said to Semer, "It is like the Lofot dikes"—because he had returned to cross with her, after he had gone over with Atwar.

He carried Atwar almost always now. The boy could stand on his splinted leg, but it was growing together crooked, and the other one, though healed, turned in oddly below the knee. The Medical Book women talked of breaking them again, but this was put off—"At Turuk, perhaps, it could be done safely." Atwar's hip, too, was left crooked, but he felt pain, even in his feet, and they assured him this was good and to welcome it—"Your feet are alive, and are angry with you, and crying out because they want to be cured and walk." One foot, the splinted one, turned in against the splint, so he stood, awkwardly, on the side of it.

Semer was able to speak with Tasman as they rested on the bank, and ask her for the first time if she had been afraid for her sons.

"Some children saw them run back, and go in among the farms, and when we knew they were not with us, and we had searched, they came forward and told us this, and I was certain, then, they had followed you. If I was afraid, it was because I was not sure they would find you. The Sorud thought of going back, but it was then four days, and the Pechor people reasoned that they would be through the pass, and we would be better able to find them from the eastern side, if you had not come with them already, and with the Travellers."

She stopped speaking. Her voice had been clear, tired, emotionless.

"Forgive-us."

"Because you ask me, but it would be better to thank you."

They embraced, and held each other, and she kissed his face through the mass of wet, scratchy hair that half hid it.

"Atwar—" he said.

"Ah—he lives, and I think even, he would not have missed all that. They are making a tale of it already."

Semer released her and sat back.

"It was not an adventure. It was ugly. It will never be as a tale."

"Maybe none of the tales were otherwise," she said quietly. "People change them so, to tame them. My mothers told many, many tales, and they were very ugly, most of them, if you thought of it—"

They lay down, and their soaked shirts cooled their bodies, and the stars shone, because the night was moonless, and the river whispered. Betwar waded past close to them with a burning branch, calling out to Atwar where he sat a little farther upstream behind some bushes. They heard the noise of the children with him, cracking twigs and branches and chattering, and the more distant voices of people on the river. The fire caught, crackling, and Atwar's laugh rang out, a bright, clear sound.

Semer watched them moving in the unsteady firelight beyond the bushes. Then he turned away and looked at Tasman, lying on her side in her fashion with her eyes lowered, an elbow under her head. He thought he would tell her about the night on the dikes, and how it had seemed to him that he had heard her voice, but before he could decide how to begin, she was asleep.

At Turuk the people spoke another speech, and those of the moving city saw among them for the first time eastern people with narrow heads—because it was their custom to bind the malleable heads of their newborn children, up to two years of age, to shape them. They were taller and seemed stronger than the western people, and they all had sleek hair and pulled it close to their heads. The bones of their inward cheeks and temples were deformed and flattened, so they had an austere, upright posture; they looked, at first glance, as though strong sunlight behind them or distance had narrowed them. The women kept the palms of their hands bald by rubbing them with certain stones, which they carried constantly; these palms were very pale, almost white, and some of them coloured their bald palms with a reddish dye, and some older women had coloured their clothing also; but to the western people it looked as if they had been hurt, and Betwar hated it.

The Ve stayed close to them, and told them what they said, changing it into true speech. They were guided through a long street in the shade of a continuous housewall, and in the centre of the city were taken up onto a house made of earth and wood. There was an open space around it, like a great market, but clean, and here many hundreds of people came to look at Tasman and her sons—their looks were kind. Also, they sat and lay down in groups on the ground, and some of them told what must have been songs and tales.

All the young children, including the Avskel, were brought among the children of Turuk to receive the speech. Tasman by an effort began to learn it, there and on their journey; but Twel Sorud had received it already, as a gift from the Ve, because his mind, in the receiving of speech, was "clear as the minds of children."

Twel showed the bit of true book to scholars at Turuk, and they studied it together, but the scholars could not explain it to him. However, they told him that between Turuk and the southern and western part of Manj'u there was a vast, high desert lying between Savannah and Sheath, and most of it was sand, not stone: "and there are people who know its northern peripheries, whom we can ask about these things."

But at Turuk there was no more news from the east. They had no Medical Book either, although perhaps they had wisdom enough, because they dissuaded the Novaya Zemlya women from interfering with Atwar's legs. They said, "He will be lame, but he is in less pain now and no fever, and the skin had shut its mouth against you and does not desire this." So they left his body alone, except for the splint of stems, and he began to try to walk after a fashion, because he was determined in it.

From there and east of that city there were no cars. There were many parallel roads, very wide, one beside the other, because the ground was soft and they pulled wood along them on wheeled rafts, from the forests, not thinking it unseemly to cut trees. Whenever the ruts became too deep, they abandoned that road, and they had done this since before they could remember, for many generations. So the city walked eastward in the ruts, many abreast, with many from Turuk travelling with them, and their children.

They reached Baikit in advanced Darkening, with no more young deaths and no adventures, except that the moon's wind increased in strength and the earth shook when it passed, and at other times. The huge land was open to the south of them, and to the north were the beginnings of forests. There were some small cities, and all the people they met, or who joined them, had shaped heads. Semer carried Atwar almost always, although the Sorud also carried him when he asked.

At Baikit were men who knew the desert they would pass, and the Sorud talked with them, inside one of the joined houses, all squatting around a well, because in these cities they had the habit of building their houses over their wells, or over pitpools. There was a river under the city.

"We have seen how the desert moves, in the moon's wind—the sand is heavy, in steep hills, and the peak or point of them is sometimes like a tip of flame and when the wind passes, it spins it out like a braid or a thread, and if this sand strikes you, it could knock you down, and it whines."

"Does the earth shake?"

"As here, more and more frequently. We have seen hills cut, as with a knife."

Semer broke in: "This city is no safe place, built on water as it is, with the world becoming more and more restless." He put out his hands, and drew Atwar and Betwar back from the lip of the well.

Twel asked, in their eastern speech, "Is that desert too dangerous to enter?"

"What reason is there to enter it? Farther south towards the Sheath, it is as the Sheath, there is nothing. In some cities near this edge, people go into it a short distance, for certain plants."

"It might be necessary to enter it, to find something we must find."

Semer repeated, in the real speech, "This city is not safe. Let us leave it." And his stomach lurched.

The earth jumped, shivered. They went outside quickly, and all the other people came out of their houses as well, calling to each other.

They travelled from there to a place called Yar, and the wind blew almost without pause, sometimes in great gusts, and always against them. Till Yar the country had been much the same, a grassy Savanna with round low hills, and seeps in the bottoms, where water could be pressed up into their cloths. At Yar they were told, "There are no more cities unless you walk directly north, and past those hills in the south-east is the desert." So the Sorud decided to remain at Yar, hoping that the people living on those peripheries could help them.

Semer lay in Yar in the short day, stretched out behind a continuous housewall, in the shade, half asleep. The moon in daylight hung overhead, creamy gray, and it seemed that within its most limited, dull tonality, innumerable detail, which was just too small to register, was visible. Turning his head aside, he saw how his Twar's gaze was also fixed on it, how the pace of his blinking slowed as he stared, and sometimes halted, and that again large tears stood in his eyelashes. Simultaneously he felt the sickness in their body, and sprang up, and called out to the city, "Wake up! and come out, the world is going to quicken!"

Those who heard him, and the ones they warned, came out, and were unhurt, but this was a large tremor, like a wave passing, and like a sighing. Some houses fell in and many people were hurt, but none were killed. Semer ran and saw Tasman standing with earth on her, near a house: the side of it had caved inward, and in the earth was a knife-cut; then Atwar pulled himself out of the roof, dirty and laughing, and Betwar climbed out after him.

33

In the sand lies half buried
a great lens, of
fragile glass, scratched
by the sand and the wind

S emer Twel wakened suddenly in great terror, and
looked around him, for he was not in Yar. And he
had no idea where he was, or how he had come there.
He was standing upright in a strange, peaky desert—
steeply graded hills with no vegetation, all of a dark,
smooth grayish colour with long parallel wrinkles in
the surface, as in cloth, it looked as if the land were
covered with cloth. The hills were not large, some no
larger than a house, but every hill's tip was pointed. It
was dark. Stars shone. It was silent.

Semer sat down, still terrified. He clasped and felt
his feet, pushing his thumbs into them, and found
them tender and tired, with the foothair tangled. He
was hungry, but his bundles were not on his arms or
thighs, only the knife bound to his upper arm. He had
lain down to sleep, in the morning, in Yar—

His hands felt at the dark sand around him. In the
starlight, he could make out the tracks of his feet, trail-
ing off behind him and out of sight between two hills
—one wavering set of tracks. He was so convinced

that no others were near that he did not think to call out. He was alone in his body with his brother.

He inhaled deeply. His fear subsided and some sense of ordinary well-being returned with his breath, and he stood up. To go back, in the cool of darkness, following the tracks, would not be difficult, as it was only midnight; his body could not have walked longer than half a day. Filled with baffled concern and wonder, he took a step northward.

And was halted in it. His surprise made him fall down, it was as if he had walked against a wall. At the same time, a tender idea of the funniness of his situation made him almost laugh. He was kneeling. He tried a giggle—aloud, and then said sternly, "Twar!"

He looked askance at his brother. Then, cautiously, he tried to lift his Twel arm, and found he was able to, and with it he touched his brother's face, pushing aside the bush of hair that as usual hid his profile. The Twar face revealed nothing extraordinary. He turned it to him and it followed, without resistance. "What are you doing to us?" he asked, and giggled again, helplessly. Those dull eyes—and when he released it, the head swivelled forward again as if mechanically. But then he felt their body stood up and turned resolutely to face the south.

The following hours were spent rolling and scrambling in that depression between the hills, the silence broken only by Semer Twel's half desperate shouts and giggles, and then the rising whine of blowing sand. Finally, as the late dawn spread over the scene, they set off in the only direction Semer found it possible to walk in, southeast towards the rising sun. As the wind strengthened, long, parallel threads of sand tweeled away off the tips of the hills that the wind was ever building and dissipating. The air vibrated on a series of high, wavering notes, endlessly drawn-out interweaving chords and discords, and the pale pink-blue of the lower sky was crossed by innumerable gray, horizontal lines, like lines drawn across a screen. And suddenly, there, close by as his body walked between the next hills, he saw what they had come for.

When the others, following the footprints, came to the place, they found the Semer seated with back turned, slumped over forward and motionless, and beyond them the huge, translucent wedge of a glass disc, as wide as a city, rearing up in a curved wall out of sand that had half buried it.

Tasman cared for them, in a cool house in Yar, and they recovered, but the first words Semer Twel spoke were "Watch us!" She did not immediately understand, but later, he told her how their body had walked away in sleep, and that this had made him very afraid.

"I do not know," he said, half sitting up and allowing her again to wipe his face, "if it is my mind in sleep; I think it cannot be, because of how I fought for our body. If it is my brother, there is not enough strength in me to withstand him." He laughed. "In one way, I feel happy about this, as if he could not really harm us. But, Tasman, he walked without water."

"*A tree opens to the light, and has its own purposes,*" said Tasman softly. She wiped the Twar face, allowing herself to look into it, though there was no response.

The city remained all this time around Yar, in shelters, and in the houses they considered secure. The Sorud needed many people with them for the work of clearing the disc, and the work was very difficult, and at first appeared almost impossible.

They found, however, that the properties of the sand were also beneficial. In mass it was solid even though it was so fine, and very heavy; and they were able, as they dug the disc free, to protect the lens with a heavy bank to the east, which was the direction the wind blew in. So they moved hills, sometimes using their rugs for rafts, and a large road came into being where the Semer footprints had gone, between Yar and that valley. They worked almost continuously, except when the earth shook or the wind was too strong. Even by keeping in the lowest places, they could not avoid the whips of sand when they blew, and many people's faces and arms were bruised, but they were learning to dodge them. It was a short way, no more than half a day's walk, from the ordinary land near Yar, so people could come out and rest, and there were those who carried food and water. At Yar, the people who had been hurt in the houses also worked if they could, to make bags and tools, and they cared for each other.

Tasman cared for the Semer, and her sons when they would let her, and learned from the Avskel more of the language they had received, but Twel Semer called it unspeech, and she did not succeed in persuading him to learn any of it.

"Whatever it is we are going towards, it will be in Lofot in the high lands we-Semer will live at last, if we live; and if there is a time to speak then, it will be in the true speech."

He looked into her narrow face. Her eyes under the heavy browline were as always, black as slate and serious. What lay ahead of them, where were they going? And, as if he could not bear to look ahead, his mind clung to the brink of the present, to these days, as she took care of him, with their tangible troubles and pleasures, while she was still with them—if he could not bear to think of it, how could she, who was and would be the reason and the solving?

He stammered, and said as carefully as he could, "Do you think much about these new things, Tasman, or do you simply allow them to happen as they happen?"

She went on with her task, wringing cloths, cooling his and his brother's temples.

"Ah—both, because if I thought of it too much, I would be afraid. The city, and all the world's people, are turning their fear into joy because of me, but I have no decision in it. I am not myself their salvation —"

"But through you, they will find it, you believe this."

"—Do you?" It sounded like a child's question in its suddenness and directness.

"No—not as they do," said Semer immediately. "I know you are an ordinary person."

Her eyes rested on his for a moment. Then she got up and went to the door, and stared into the daylight with its ponderous moon, and her eyes filled with tears.

34

*The correlate, the counterpart
is the impossible*

A s they had nearly finished clearing the sand from
the lens, a large group appeared from the east,
people who had come out to meet them. The people
from Yar brought them into the desert, and Betwar
ran ahead, and stood beside his fathers in that valley,
when they came walking towards them across the
levelled sand.

They were tall, both men and women, made even
taller by their sleek, gleaming hair that was pulled
tightly high up on their shaped heads. Like the eastern people who had already joined the city, they had
hairless brows and temples, and shallow eyes. Their
skin was cool, almost bluish. These people wore
tunics of very fine, thin cloth, that the sun had
bleached very pale, with a single, wide sleeve.
Between the heads of some of them was a vertical,
stiffened cloth, that came forward between their
shaped cheeks, but the meaning of this was not clear.
Their tunics were very full, and open at the sides, and
they had long gloves on their feet. Some of them carried almost nothing, or nothing, and others too much.
There were no children with them.

Those with the greatest burdens put them down, and came forward and greeted the Sorud. They spoke clearly and slowly in their own speech, and Twel told his brother the meaning of everything they said.

"We are called Azur, and have run from the Book at Manj'u, expecting to meet you. Our letter is to Tasman and is *Come quickly* and so we have said it. At Turuk we met Travellers who turned with us and ran with us back to Yar, telling us to come just as quickly to this place, and see what you have found. Will you look at it with us?"

Twel said earnestly: "Then speak to us first of Manj'u, so that we know everything you know. We have only heard the old letter, and have many questions."

At that, because of his evident authority, the Azur called women to them, who walked with them and answered Twel, but they themselves did not answer him. They gestured impatiently to Betwar to keep close to them, and looked about for others to speak to, turning their body jerkily so they both could see, because of the stiffened cloth between them. Betwar tugged at Twar's sleeve and said, "Fadar, they are looking around at the people," so Twar began to speak to them patiently, and answer their questions.

They were old Tellers, he reasoned, for whom a learned letter, or any other knowledge, was rote and tedious. Their curiosity (like Twel Sorud's) had overcome any sense of obligation to tell what they knew. As for Twel, his only desire was to learn, he had no patience for talking about the disc, which was, after all, before their own eyes.

They walked together under the steep inner rim of the disc as it rose out of the deep depression, and the Azur gazed up at it, and touched it with their long, bluish fingers.

Concave, it leaned back skyward, and held the hot morning light as in a great sleeve, and the sun caught at its upper rim in a curved arc too bright to look at. Its lower rim was still buried, and the people who had stopped work to look at the newcomers had again begun their digging; as the Azur watched, some ran down the broken slopes of the hollow to pull away rafts full of sand that had been dug close to the disc. Others scooped at the sand, turning it back and loading another raft—it looked darker, and cool.

"There is burnt-sand here," said the Twel Azur, their hand slipping over the surface. He had spoken in his own speech, which Twar Sorud barely understood.

"He means, glass within glass." Betwar, his round face serious, was telling Twar what he had said.

"It has been much scratched by the sand and wind," said Twar to them. "It is perhaps fragile despite its great size and thickness. We are trying to back it and protect it with sand, as we reveal its face, and if its shape is as it predicts itself it will be perfect, a perfect disc of glass tilted toward the southern sky." Again, Betwar told them what he had said.

"But you are blind."

"I have touched it and learned it. And my sons see for me also. But you will see for yourselves, that the back of it is as plain as the front, without any door or seam, and set solidly on a heavy foundation, that is all made immovable out of something that feels like the feel of the Sheath, and they say it is absolutely black, and reflects nothing, and goes directly in to the earth farther than it is possible to discover. There is nothing else here—no ruins of any kind."

"It is the world's face," said Azur Twar, still gazing upward, "and the moon will be persuaded into abasement before her—she will not turn at all towards him."

Betwar, stammering, said to his father, "Twar, they are talking about asking the moon to get down in front of the disc—I think."

"Well, it is certain that the disc will not move, except with the world."

The Azur walked slowly eastward in front of the disc's base, stepping fastidiously around the people who were digging, and looked behind it where the sand was now stacked high against its forbidding overhang. Betwar, following them, did not like to stare up at it, though from there he could not see its forward-curving lip—it was too like the cliff of the earthfall, and (as far as he could remember) just as high.

Twel Sorud said meanwhile to the women, "Tell us about the lake which is like a mirror in Manj'u. I have been wondering, perhaps it looks like this." His voice broke with excitement.

"No, it is not like this," said the women, their Twar speaking first, the Twel continuing. "It is much smaller, and contained in metal in a long cradle, lying as the bone lies within the arm, and turns at the shoulder."

"Why is it called a lake?"

"To look into it is to look into a lake, and the moon fills it, clearing and making understandable to us his expression and all its details. The lake walks across the surface of the moon like the eye of children walking across their mothers' faces. At our Book, we have two true linear pictures, correspondences, that are very old, but we have copied them (there have been scholars who spent their whole lives copying them), and one corresponds to what we see, in every particular, except that now the fruit of the seed has covered everything that is covered."

The Sorud sat down, and from then on did not move, and Twel made the women sit with them, until they had answered everything that he asked. But their speech seem curious and convoluted to his western ears—they seemed to prefer to speak in pictures, and at times, even though he was sure he understood every word, he was more confused by their answers than he had been before he asked. Also, he discovered that they themselves were not perfectly knowledge-able; the scholars who had told them the letter were at Manj'u waiting, and these Travellers had been sent because they were the fastest runners, and knew the way.

Twel Sorud placed his fist between their breasts. "What can you tell us, that I have not asked?" he said in a louder voice. "The world is so restless now, we know the time is short, but we do not know. Is there any new information among you?"

"Perhaps there is, but we do not know it."

"Have you no other letters with you from Manj'u?"

"Only those words we greeted you with: *Come quickly.*"

The Twar woman said, "Before we were brought to you, when we stood before Tasman in Yar, she told us the meaning of this lens, as it was written in the fragment of true book that was found. It is the correl-ative."

"Yes," said Twel impatiently. "It is prepared for these times, surely, and its purpose is benevolent, but in our ignorance we could have lost it—we could still lose the moment of its direction."

"Ah—it goes deep! straight to the barycentre," said the Twar woman in a rare direct statement. "It will take care of itself and what it must do, whether we care or not."

"It is the moon that must be enticed," added her twin enigmatically. Twel had difficulty reading their faces, which seemed to him obliterated of meaning, like the interim-masks of Tellers in the market.

The Sorud stood up, and Twel said, "I will not question you further, but think about what you have told me. We will prepare to go quickly with you. The lens stands cleared by tomorrow, and what protection we can give it is completed, by making the ground level to the east, and by banking it. We are ready."

Meanwhile, at Yar, Semer, slowly recovered from his starvation, waited as patiently as he could, and learned all that was said to Tasman, and what Sorud Twel told her, and wondered whether, when they went on to Manj'u, his body would allow him to go with them. Because he had some idea of sitting again and facing that disc, alone, as he had been made to do before, because of his Twar's incomprehensible authority, and of dying there. But he reasoned that he could ask to be bound and carried east, if it came to the worst. And since that one time, he had not felt anything more from his brother, except that, just as before, their body sickened when the earth was about to quake, and the Twar wept.

35

"We can restore your sight. It is like glass set into a roof, so the people in the house can see out, but the glass is smoked. We cannot clean it. The eye wants to see but the glass, by which we mean, the skin of the eye, is clouded. This is why you say you are blind. You are not blind. But your eye needs another skin—a clean, clear window."

"Can this be done? How can it be done?" asked Twel sharply. "I do not doubt that you can do it—"

"The old skin must be peeled away. To do this, we must hold the eye carefully in our hands. Then another skin, a clear window, is laid across the naked surface of the eye, and made fast, which we do by burning it, and the eye is gently replaced in its little bowl of bone. It would not be painful for the eye, because of very strong plants we will give you to eat. Then you could look again out of the window, and your mind's house receive the immaculate light of the world."

Twar asked, stammering, "Where is this clear skin to be found?"

"On the eye of your brother."

Manj'u was a great, rich country, and the city Fu-en full of brilliant colours and contrasts, and noise and variation. The water of the Sea of Peace poured twice a day through its deep channels, and the roofs were covered with flowering trees. The people were weavers, and hung the whitening and red-dipped sheets of their cloth everywhere in the sunlight, they stretched it into housewalls and lay in its hammocks and under its shade, and it streamed in the moon's wind, and often pieces of it were seen caught in the trees, or loosened, blowing across the city. They ate the meat of many fruits other than the hips, and ripe fruit as orange as blood, and their farms extended into the forests, where the people lay down, and stretched their naked arms into the pools, and pulled up edible roots, some white and some black.

But the edges of the city, towards the water, were cracked open, and many new houses had been destroyed by certain waves, that came after the sea ran away farther and faster than with ordinary tides—so you could see, they said, the "old city" on the shelf of the sea bed, before those greater waves. When it was seen, people ran up to the higher ground. There was a watch set, day and night. But such a wave had not come, since the western city's arrival.

The Fu-en scholars wished to take Tasman away from her family, immediately, but they deferred to Sorud Twel, and because of him she remained with the others; they were given a cloth-walled house in a group of white houses joined around a central court, on the highest hill in the city. People brought them food, and some of it they ate, but some they did not like, and the water was also strange, being clean but heated and very dark. However, there was clear water to wash in, and they drank that. The Fu-en people also brought them sun-whitened garments of the thin cloth, which Tasman liked, because they were so light and cool. She persuaded the others to wear them too, but she could not persuade Semer. Many hundreds of people came to look at her there.

They had hardly slept, when they heard the noise of stamping on the ground, and her sons pulled back a cloth-wall and saw the Fu-en people climbing the narrow streets. Some, at the front, knew how to blow into stems of wood, and the sound reminded Tasman of the Bogdan-a telling, but was more intricate, high and breathy. One twin would blow and the other punctuate it by knocking forehead or wrist against the wood. They walked in a certain manner, and blew and stepped, the others' steps copying theirs, so it was like a tale with no words, the people following it to listen to it, and then coming nearer and staring at the Avskel peeking out of the house-wall. All night their blowing, and the whispering of their unspeech and the shuffle of their gloved feet moved around the house, and sometimes a wall rippled when a hand inadvertently touched it.

The Sorud had gone in to Book immediately without sleep, and their body was feverish with the Twel's great desire to see everything, and to understand what he saw. Book was south of the city, where the Sheath—which was very high, higher than the city's highest hill—seemed to pour itself like a steep, smooth and glistening black wave into the endless ocean to the east. Perhaps because of the water, the Sheath was fairly cool here, even in Lightening, but no one went on it. Under it were great bays extending southward and inland, where the sea ran far in. In places, the people had built against the incursion of the water; some of this damming up, they were told, had been done in ancient times. The Sheath's swelling surface was broken with smooth-edged holes and depressions, like the whirlpools seen in standing waves, and deep inside, like another city, the great Book of Manj'u extended under the gleaming roof—where once the sea had boiled and withdrawn, and where, in bursts of scalding steam, it had forced back the liquid Sheath like shore-mud shaped in its hardening. Now daylight or moonlight streamed through the natural openings, and under one, near the centre, stood the lake of the moon.

The Sorud and the others had not understood what was told them at Yar, for they had imagined looking inside an instrument of singular delicacy, like an eye, with the moon's detail walking on it for one eye to see. Instead, they found that there was indeed a kind of made lake—though it contained no water—and on its flat, dull surface projected what the arm-eyed instrument received, when it was turned towards the sky. The Sorud were shown how, by extending it joint by joint, out of the smooth socket of its shoulder, parts of the sky overhead could be projected on the lake floor, and how, as it was extended or contracted, less or more of the sky appeared. The lake floor itself was perfectly round, and sunken, and at its edge was a low barrier, all the way around it. Twel Sorud saw how the people knelt and folded their arms along it, so they could lean forward and look into the lake without falling. He was told that the scholars climbed down by a set of shallow steps, and walked on it, and made dark marks, by dragging a stick of ash, on strips of cloth that had been laid out, and then folded the cloth and carried it up, to store it in Book and look at it. They had assembled these cloths since the beginning of the unclouding of the moon, and there was great detail on them, and all the changes.

But it was moonless the first time they looked at the lake, so they did not yet see this demonstrated.

In all that part of Book were constructions whose meaning was unknown to the Sorud, and they found that the meaning of many of them was also unknown to the Fu-en people. There were machines whose sides were as smooth as the Sheath itself; some had the seams of joins and doors on them, but so close-set the people could not prize a knife or a fingernail into them, and they had no handles of any kind. Some looked almost exactly like screens—and there were many—but they were blind and dirty, and where the keys should have been was only a smooth-topped box, and no visible way of opening it. It was obvious that the scholars held all these things in veneration; Sorud Twel was less awed, he thought he would surely have got one apart by now even if it were broken in the process. But he could tell they would not have let him.

"We are not sure of its purpose and we have not learned to set it in motion," or, "It is part of the journey," were the answers Twel often received. Farther in, the Sheath was broken in many places, smoothly but randomly, and under one of these openings, rising out of the centre of another round, deep floor like a lake, was the largest and most complex of the constructions. It was black and seamless except, high-up and reached by a laddered stair, was the outline of a simple, narrow door. The Fu-en people told them, "Inside is a car within a car and its design and proportions are written in the First Script and in there is the screen, that our letter told you of. But we will teach you everything we know."

Then Tasman, with ceremony, was robed in the skin of the snake, to be taken into Book. She had seen how the Fu-en people deferred to some among them, but this did not seem to be in recognition of any personal authority (as it was with Sorud Twel) because both twins of a pair were treated just the same, and they were not "true twins" either. It seemed to her uncouth and unnecessary. Those who commanded the most respect wore the stiffened cloth between their faces. But she could discern no particular merit in them that should have set them apart. Twel had told her only one pair among the scholars wore the cloth board, and they were not the brightest, though they always spoke first.

One pair, the Wan, women who seemed among the most powerful of all, entered the house after a certain amount of blowing and walking around it with a large crowd, and regarded her directly as was their way. Tasman—like Twel and others she had talked to among the western people—could not read their faces, or easily tell them apart; but Twar had said, "Perhaps they find our faces as alike, and difficult to understand, as we find theirs."

But life among them, despite their grace and quickness, would have a serious cast, she thought, because of their needless ceremonies and their seemingly dazed or distant look. She had, however, noticed that their children laughed, even the little bandaged twins whose heads they had not finished shaping.

The Wan carried before them an oblong vessel full of white clay, which they set down on the floor inside the threshold, and the young women who had robed her came forward and crouched beside it. The Wan indicated, by a slight stooping of their body, that Tasman should crouch too. They were still looking at her directly out of their shallow eyes. It was hard to see their warped inner eyes at the proximity; these slid half around the flat-side of their faces.

When she squatted, the women dipped one finger into the clay and painted a vertical line up the centre of her face, from under her chin up over the crown of her head. She winced at the cold touch of the clay but the Sorud were behind her, and Twel advised her to allow this: "It is meant for a sign of your power, I think, like the stiffened cloths are for them, and for the Travellers who met us in Yar."

Semer was sitting against one wall, pleased with the sheen of the skin she was at last wearing, but he scowled when they marked her—he could almost feel his own face tighten and tingle.

Atwar, coming close, asked the women who painted Tasman, dipping their finger again into the chalky clay, retracing the line on her face: "Why do you do this? and what is the reason for those white board?"

They answered, "They enforce obedience."

Then Atwar and Betwar, who had chattered to the women earlier and were at ease with them, began to play with the clay and—as is recorded in the Tale— Betwar drew a line down Atwar's face, but the women stopped them, and wiped away the mark.

When the clay was dry, Tasman was taken into Book, the Sorud with the Avskel following, and around them a large throng hurried down the hill by the many streets, and gathered and stopped at the entrances. Tasman saw what the scholars had already shown the Sorud, and stayed till morning looking at the cloth maps, as they were unfolded and folded, learning the directions, waiting for the moon so she could she see for herself.

She was also shown the true book they called the First Script, which contained line traces of the inside of the car, that they said they could not get into themselves, because it was, in spite of its outward size, very narrow and small at the centre. Only this central car, they said, would complete the journey.

Sorud Twel quickly understood the thought of the Outdead in what they had contemplated, though in some things, the Outdead had seemed to take for granted knowledge he could not have, and anticipated conclusions he would never have expected. But the steps were there, and he was now as convinced as the scholars at Fu-en that the ancient wisdom of the Outdead had not only made the moon habitable, but had also invented a delicate procedure to prevent Moonfall. No one knew all that it entailed, beyond this first necessary journey.

When the moon again appeared in the sky, they knelt night after night at the barrier, with Betwar clambering and Atwar hanging perilously over it with his strong arms clutching it, and saw its great white shape waver into focus below them, and the picture move, from distant to close, and then swing sideways giddily as though they hovered over it like a sheet of cloth lifted and drifting on the wind.

They saw the edge of the canals, and the great spaced arches bowing across them, and their shadows on the unbroken foliage below. They saw how the transparent skin or covering, whatever it was, was puckered at the arches, as if it were soft rather than hard, and bound or melted into them—and on its surface, as the moon's face swung below them, were puckerings that looked as if it had been torn and melted together again. Some boulders lay on it, deep, as if in hammocks of cloth, and the Fu-en scholars told them that these were like the stones that had marked the moon. They saw, as the image swung to the left, how the canal opened in to the Sea of Rains, and how the network of the bowed bridges became more intricate as it spread out over the trees. And they saw,

finally, at the Terminator, the sward or amphitheatre
that some children had been able to see with the
naked eye since the clouds had lifted—a bright,
smooth blue, with markings across it that might have
been paths or traces, and the low, squared surfaces of
buildings to one side. On the roof of the largest building two signs were written, unaltered letters of the
First Script in the old eastern speech. The second sign
was clear enough to read: 友 which means
friend.

36

Tasman withdrew into herself after she had learned
these things and spent most the time sitting alone
in a corner of the house while the others slept or were
at Book. The white-sheeted walls and her white gar-
ment glimmered by daylight or moonlight, or in the
dim yellowish gleam of a lamp placed at a distance;
her arms were black with their two white bracelets of
bone. Semer saw her there, and sometimes came over
to her, but she did not acknowledge him, though
sometimes he sat near her, in silence, in those hours.

He had been walking, and came to her there one
morning. She was sitting on her old human hair rug,
and moved a little so he could sit down beside her.

"Tasman, you have been alone with your mind for many days now, and I was also alone in my mind. I am here to tell you what is going to happen."

"Ah—I know that already," she said calmly. "I am not afraid."

He shifted, so he could look into her quiet face, where the last bits of clay still clung to the centre of her eyebrows and to her hair.

"Tasman, listen. In the days of the Outdead, the men who made those plans and looked into the sky— they went there also, as we always half-believed—we know it now, though they never lived there long, for the moon was airless then and terrible, but they must have gone there many times, and done many things. They made the great bridges across the canals and connected them with that fabric we have seen, that shining roof, and covered the Sea of Rains and the Sea of Quiet, and the lesser seas, and the Lake of Death. And they created inside them the sources of continuous winds of air, and left seeds that would bear fruit and make the air sweet, after three thousand Darkenings. And they calculated the orderly descent of the moon in perfect and impeccable harmony. And invented how it could be stopped in its path and turned to the right way. And I think there were men and women among them, whose lives were made happy in doing these things—not just the scholars, but the ones who travelled also, and who walked on the moon and thought how it would be."

He paused for breath, and she seemed about to answer him, or perhaps stop him, so he went on hurriedly:

"The one who ought to go is the one whom it would delight, not the one who says, 'I am ready,' or, 'I am not afraid.'"

She sighed. "Can you teach me that delight? And these Fu-en people, they see me as a mirror, a screen, one of the Outdead whose Book they have studied in all their generations. So I have to be this, even if you know I am not—and called me ordinary." She smiled. "I have to be what the world says I am. And I am, ready."

She was silent, and he put his urgent hand on her arm.

"Me, Tasman. I am the one it will delight. I ache for it." And when she stared, he added softly, "Trees sometimes must be felled. Even to make a splint for Atwar—remember?—we had to fell a tree."

So Sorud Twar received the skin of his brother's eye, and the Twel's joy in the giving was almost greater than the Twar's in the receiving of it. After this, the Fu-en people, who were very clever in such things, intended to heal Atwar's legs, and it was even told in the Tale (*They would have caused Atwar to grow / As tall as other men, / Healers of blindness, / Blind to his beauty*).

But they refused to listen to Semer, first because they were determined for Tasman, and second because they believed there was not enough time. So he went to some other men, secretly, who because of something they had done were not of that Book any more, and in his desperation convinced them—and they would have done it, but when they had learned the measurements of the entrance to the cars, and their inner circumference, they also refused, and told him, "You would still be unable to enter, and therefore it said in the letter, *It is a woman*." Semer mourned.

As he was returning from his last fruitless visit with them (they lived northwest of the city, against a marsh-forest) in the morning, passing along a narrow street of white and pale red walls, he felt his body suddenly halted, as if he had walked into a tree. Glancing at his brother he saw the familiar tears, and their stomach lurched as it did before the earth shook. He tried to move but could not. No one was about—it was already hot and people slept—but he shouted with all his voice's strength. The city began to answer, people running outside, some naked, calling to waken the more distant streets. They ran uphill past him, hardly taking time to stare, escaping to the high ground in the centre of the city. Semer, rooted, heard the watchers at the shore take up the warning and blow piercingly through their wooden stems as they ran.

After that it was eerily still, and deserted where he was, (he stood on low ground, near a canal) though the air jittered.

Then he heard a great rushing sound, as the water fled out of the canals seaward, and after that a huge quake rolled the earth under his feet and threw him violently down.

The housewall next to him was torn from top to bottom with a shriek, and the house splintered. The air was suddenly full of dust and shreds; and then the wind came, and then the water.

But he lived, because he was outdoors and nothing fell on him. He was hurled by the water farther inland, and when its wave withdrew, he stayed where he was, on a hill, washed up within the beam of a house. The people hiding on the hill found him. The old bruise reappeared on his side, but he was otherwise unharmed.

They tended him among the tatters of their house, and he let them bind up his side (which was the only time he submitted to the white cloth), but he refused to stay, and hurried across the ruins of the city without stopping, till he got to the Sorud house.

The hill houses had withstood, and the Sorud lay sightless indoors as he had left them—because their eyes were still bound at the time—and their sons lay asleep at their feet. Staring about, he could see beyond them the shadow of Tasman, unmistakable among other shadows, moving and stooping behind a cloth-wall that blazed in the sunlight.

"Sorud!" he said to them both, for their profiles, under the white and red bands, were equally removed and austere.

"We are listening to you, Twel Semer," said the Twel. "We have heard that you called out before the quake. Our sons have been outside, they saw the wave and have been crawling about everywhere for hours—they were brought to us safe, with hurt children they had found—Tasman is with people from Medical Book caring for the people. Where were you, that it took you so long to return?"

Semer came very close to them, stammering. "Ah —we went secretly to men who would have done what I wanted, and quickly. I think you know what that was. But they are convinced that this body, even mutilated, could not enter the cars, they have shown me the measures." He began to sob, and once begun could not control it, and as he leaned over them they felt the hot salt of his tears on their faces, through the scratchy mass of his hair. He lay in the arms of the Sorud and wept.

"Ah—we cannot alter anything, that was determined so long ago," said Twel almost to himself. Semer's decision had broken in upon his resignation strangely—almost, he had felt a need to argue against it, because his love for his housebonded lay like a fragile grain of light in the spacious reaches of the times his mind moved in, and was utterly coloured by the inevitability of what he had prepared her for. But the Twar's rush of hope, when Semer offered himself, was almost as desperate as Semer's own. He, also, would not have thought it strange to take her place if he could, his mind would have made that journey in delight.

Sight was returned to him, and when they unwound the bands, his son Atwar's black face was before him, pinched with pain and laughing with the white teeth of childhood. And Betwar's, pushing in close beside him, softer and rounder, his sons that he had never seen. And Tasman then, whose touch and voice through those years had taught him to know her now—tired, quiet, steady, beautiful, an adult woman.

He saw also the Semer Twel for the first time, his fairness and his surprising youth—for the Semer looked more like boys than men—and his Twar's empty gaze, the dull eyes behind the thick white lashes.

Then he turned to his brother, recognized his bruised face with a pang of joy, and asked, "Do you see?" and the Twel smiled, and kissed him: "half as well as I am used, and twice as well—for I see you seeing." So they stood up, and Twar wondered at everything he looked on.

37

This is what happened: Atwar went, because it was not possible for Tasman, either, to enter the cars. There was wild crying out and terror around the lake floor, when it was finally realized she could not, but Atwar grinned.

These primitive people kissed him, and bound food and water to his arms and his small, misshapen legs, as if he were going for a walk on the Savannas of the earth, not believing that his every possible need would be satisfied. They took charcoal and wrote the directions into the palms of his two bald hands, though he squirmed and insisted he knew them. He entered the instrument of his journey barefoot, scrambling up the ramp and squeezing through the tiny, narrow door. When it closed, the lights went out around it, and other lights appeared under it, and the whole structure began to shudder. Some of the scholars panicked and ran back towards the lake and the part of Book nearer Fu-en, but others took things more calmly, and walked. An iron wall closed behind them, and they were separated from Atwar.

Trembling, the whole population of Fu-en and the walking city stood on the southern slopes of the hill, among the broken and standing houses, looking south, with no stem-noise or shouting. The Wan stood close outside Book at the front of the throng with the scholars and other twins who wore the stiffened cloth, and with the Sorud, who held Betwar and Tasman tightly in their arms; but Semer's body ranged along the line, bright-haired and rough-dressed in brown, the only restless one, breathing hard and coughing with unspent energy, passing in front of the Wan and careless of their forbidding faces.

They could see the Sheath surface, black under the stars, with a new glow rising from it where it was broken, and they could still hear the trembling, that grew louder. As they looked, they saw a great burst of fire, and a roaring flame, higher and louder than any of them had ever imagined possible, leaped from the Sheath into the sky, and burst, and burst again, and past it a tiny light, like a star, soared across the blackness and disappeared.

38

it is
necessary that we do not know
exactly what we do
exactly where we stand

A twar reached the moon safely, as the tale tells, while in the Book at Manu'j, instruments no one had understood before came alight, and the blind surfaces of the screens slid back like the lids of eyes, and made similar pictures of him appear. They saw him try to run on the moon, and stumble, and later they saw him eat, and fall asleep in the shade of one of the buildings. The Sorud, who could not bear to turn away, and were feverish from lack if sleep—and the scholars, who were wringing their hands at the thought he would forget what he must do—saw him go down into the largest building, and saw how its lights came on shone out on the moss or grass. Just then as the lights shone out, the screens winked, and showed him indoors, concentrating, glancing at his hands and then licking them; and then touching one by one the instruments on a long panel, and smiling when they came alight.

But Tasman crouched in Book, and stared, and Betwar ran to her from the screens and back to them again, and tried to make her look at them. The Sorud saw her with sorrow, and it seemed that they had lost more than their child.

Semer's body was exhausted, and he slept all day long at the edge of Book, in the shadow of the nearest cloth-wall, its loosened fringe pulled over their faces.

The moon was now nearing perihelion, and the moon's face, huge and benign and bruised with blue, was nearly full upon the earth. As night fell the wind moaned, and shreds of the houses tore off and fled inland. Then the air stilled and the moon rose, a bell of silence. Without warning Twel Semer found his body sitting upright and in the act of fighting off the wall-sheet, then standing and—without his volition— setting off at a run towards the west.

Though he could not stop, he could call out, which gave rise to a short-lived panic in his wake; but at last, at the end of the city, three pair of strong twins understood (because everyone knew his story), snatched up water and food, and followed him as well as they could, to take care of him.

Stumbling out of the marshes, and after having fallen several times, Twel Semer gave in to his body, and allowed—instead of uselessly trying to prevent— the intention of his pounding feet. His mind slept even, in snatches, for despite his consternation he trusted his brother. They ran uphill among brown slopes on into morning. Each step pulled at their side, as when they had run to Muzh with the small weight of Atwar (this thought, an unasked gift of their body, made Twel Semer cry). They were slowing, the heat like a brown hand on their back through the heavy shirt. The bandage constricted and hurt, and he thrust his twel-hand into his sleeve and loosened it. It began to unwind and trail after, twisted and dirty, and eventually fell off. On a down-slope the Semer tripped and fell, and the first twins to catch up with them gave them water. Twel Semer bit into the soaking cloth and drank, but even as the twins tried to wet his brother's mouth, their body was up and off again, running unevenly.

Again at sundown the huge moon reared behind them, gray-light as bright as day. The moon's wind pushed them forward, along with tumbling cacti and sticks, and the dust they kicked up waist-high rolled in front of them like a myriad of cloudy stars. Then the air stilled and they slowed, labouring over small hills.

Each time they fell, some of the others caught up and sometimes were able to give them water.

"Where are you going? To the disc?" they asked in the unspeech, gasping. Semer Twel did not understand. "Rebraid our hair," he said with difficulty, between his scorched lips, and they did not understand him, either, though they were carrying the bandage and lamely offered it. But the Semer scrambled up and were away again, the frayed yellow hair-knot swinging and bumping on their shoulders.

They reached the singing desert after that day, and came to the southeast side of the valley the people made there, and threw themselves down. Twel Semer found himself freed of the running and free to move his body, and when the others came up he rolled over and drank water, but was too exhausted to eat or speak. Also, no more half-dulled, the sense of his body flooded back on him, and his eyes swam; he felt a degree of sickness that was almost lassitude, as though he would have welcomed death.

The firm earth under the sand was moving continuously now like the sea under choppy wind and, deeper, with a slow ground swell that they felt in the pits of their bellies, that lifted and lowered them, almost yearningly. The moon's wind had not stilled, but poured across them through the pointed hills, the sand's whips screaming at a pitch that was almost intolerable. All the valley they had made was changed and changing, the tracks of the rafts and the rough shapings smooth and rounded. The packed sand behind the disc had been blown clean away in long ridges and, as they watched, a long crack in the sand, and then another, opened against the disc's exposed foundation, and gaped and was filled. The whole valley floor in front was covered with tiny tipped hills, that simmered and burst and swelled up again as in a cauldron. The disc stood, it alone was motionless as the world moved, and the enormous moon, seen from the narrow head of the vale where they lay with the dark sand-peaks all around them, seemed to have swollen to the same size as the lens under it, and almost to touch its glassy surface; they inclined toward each other face to face like twins.

Then, as this opposition, at the zenith, came into exact correspondence (the watchers raised by a larger wave, and hearing an aching, unfathomable noise under them), a bar of perfect fire stood forth between the earth and the moon, so they were joined by it. It leaned with them, as in a dance, with the tension terrible and nearly beyond bearing, leaned and danced to a point beyond the moon's endurance, and he was made to submit, and turn back the infinitesimal degree that was required. After that, the bar of fire winked out, as if it had never been. And the earth quieted, being very tired.

And at Fu-en, the Sorud at the screens saw the figure of Atwar come out of the house, and cross the lawn, and go in among the trees.

They remained at Fu-en in those years, because Twar was determined to understand the instruments and how they were made, and Twel could not rest unless he could learn all there was to learn from the Book there, and with other wise men search for what was lost and not lost, so the worlds could be joined as soon as possible, even in that generation.

But the Tale says that Semer returned to Lofot, and in some versions, that Tasman went with him.

The End

Appendix: a note on language.

Moonfall was reworked from recovered texts in *Riksprok*, the language spoken in the Peninsula and called by the people there "true speech." *Riksprok* is one of the branches of the old Germanic *Nynorsk* spoken in the area at the time of the Outdead. Parts of *Moonfall*, in particular the final chapters, are prose adaptations of tales. For this reason the language may appear somewhat overpoetic, although I have taken the liberty of shortening and simplifying some of the run-on verses, and inserting direct speech.

The tales seldom describe the natural world except in utilitarian terms; people experienced it as mostly hostile, occasionally wonderful, perhaps, but never beautiful, though they had a strong sense of home. Their appreciation of beauty seems to have been reserved for the human face, and their vocabulary for facial expression is extensive and nuanced compared to English, which, while able to interpret facial expression, is ill-equipped to describe the superficial physical changes that give rise to it. In *Riksprok*, probably because of the necessity to differentiate between identical twins, expression was all important. A harmonious facial musculature was read as pleasing, or beautiful, because it was the visual sign of moral harmony (*hangsamen*), translated as "correspondence" between imagination and reality. Up to 28 superficial facial muscles are named in the true speech, while English must resort to latinisms for any but the most obvious. A few appear in the text.

Where the latinism seems awkward I have used a simplified translation.

Riksprok incorporated certain important linguistic changes to accommodate the requirements of the new society. A pair of twins (what we would call a bicephalic single human being) was called *twain* (translated "pair"). *Twain* is a dual noun: the most important development in the language being the introduction of an extra number, the dual, with its "inalienable" grammatic: while at the same time the gender singulars, with notable exceptions, virtually disappeared. Plural number applied only in reference to three or more.

The first person pronouns are *je, va* (dual), *vi*; objectives *mi, as* (dual), *os*. In common speech the objective replaces the subjective case, the verbs usually occurring without the pronoun subject and depending for the number on their endings, as: *gaa* (dual) we went, *gaau* (plural) we all went. This verb has no singular, nor does the gender verb to-be-placed (*tistad*) or to-be-present (*var/er*), although the verb for being as referring to mental states (*varsind*) has. I have tried to retain this meaning in the English —when a verb occurs in speech that has a common dual and no singular—by using italics.

Second person: *di, da* or *tha* (dual), *du; di, da*(tha), *er*. Third person: *han/hin, thay* (dual), *thom; him/hir, tham, thom*. The possessive pronouns are *min, vara/var* (dual), *vora/vor; din, dara* or *thara* (dual), *era; sin, thama* (dual), *thoma*.

Dual nouns (denoting two) usually take the ending *-as*, plurals (three or more) are irregular; usually as singular, or ending *-os*.

Past tense had no endings.

Verbs show irregularities but most verbs in present tense end as follows: singular -*i*, dual -*a*, plural -*u*, often with internal vowel changes. The future is *vil* with the present tense.

The imperative is usually the root form. Pronoun objects can form endings as forladas—"leave-us", forgivas—"forgive-us", ladmi—"allow-me".

There is no subjunctive. The fixed form *jetro* (literally, "I guess") introduces subjunctive mode.

Common phrases unfamiliar in English translation are *twarvé* (translated *to the right*) and *twelvé* (*to the left*). Nouns referring to the body, with the exception of head and neck, take the dual possessive. Although each twin was taught to use the arm/hand and leg/foot on his/her respective side of the body, applying the singular possessive was strongly discouraged: it was not polite, for example, for a twel to refer to "my hand" as *min hånd*, the proper phrase was "our twel hand"—*vara twelhånd*. Even in the unusual Sorud symbiosis, Twar would ask for courtesy-permission (*ladmi*) to begin to use both hands, etc. Dual pronouns were used for the body and dual verbs for the body's physical movement and place.

Words for persons are as follows: singular *twel* (twin left), *twar* (twin right)—capitalized as familiar names—and *sind* (I have translated this word as "mind"); dual *twain* or *twan* (translated "pair"); plural *twain* (translated "people"). A problem arises with "child/children". The dual *småa* and the plural *små* translate as "children" but there is no singular *child*. I have used "little one" for the rare singular *sindi*, a diminutive. "She never had felt like children": *Nanehin varvarsind smålika* (literally, "Not-ever-she had-been-in-mind children-like"). Similarly, the word "adult" (*voksan/vokson*) exists only in the dual and plural forms, but I have translated it as singular in referring to Tasman. "Man" and "woman", strangely enough, do have singulars (*man, kvin*): these were used, like *sind*, to refer to the individual, the "person-hood" of one twin. The duals are *manas / kvinnas* and the plurals *man* and *kvinnos*.

Words for consanguineous relationships are quite straightforward: "brother": *broder*, used as a synonym for "twin": *twin* or *twel/twar*, as was "sister": *søster*. Other siblings were called *broderas* (dual) *-os* (plural) for both sexes.

Twar: twin on the right side of the body as it faces forward. Twel: twin on the left. There was a wide-spread belief that the left-hand twin ("heartside" or *hjertsid*) was the more emotional and intuitive, the right-hand twin the more logical, but although children were expected to be so—in which case, they would perhaps tend to conform to and fulfill parental expectations—there was no physical basis for it. The Sorud were a good instance of the opposite. *Ma* (or *Mar*), *Fa* are dual nouns meaning "(both)mothers" and "(both)fathers"; the singulars are *Mamar/Mamel* and *Fadar/Fadel*.

There are extended terms for other bonds of kin-ship, for example, *mamamar* and *fafadar*, *mamamel* and *fafadel* to name and differentiate between maternal and paternal grandparents.

Tasman in referring to her body used a dual pos-sessive, as did others in referring to her, but I have translated most of her direct speech in the singular, to avoid what the reader of English would find stilted or misleading. In the ritual language of letters, her use of the dual is retained, except in the first childish letter to Lofot.

The case of Semer Twel is peculiar as he had to take complete control of the body he shared with his retarded twin. The language gives him no choice but to refer to his body, and its actions and situation, in the dual, and I have retained this in his speech, but mostly used the (to us, ordinary) singular to refer to him when he is in control: *he walked*, etc.

As for the Sorud, their agreement that Twar might control their body was very rare: it was not continuous, but Twar took over in situations where Twel was bored or abstracted, and, as we have seen, still made use of the rote-speech *ladmi* (allow-me) as a courtesy.

If forced to use the singular, as, for example, in the Saduth tale ("I am alone") or in referring to Tasman as "being-present all by herself", the genderless singular "it" (*e*) had to be used, or the archaic singular for the verb of being.

"She cannot be happy in there all by herself": this sentence contains a normal singular of *varsind* (*hin ersindi*), but in order to say "all by herself" Twar had to use the genderless singular for to-be-present (*e-eri*). The sentence *Jetro nahin ersindi glad, derind e-eri een een* means literally "I believe not-she is-present happy, therein it-is-present one (of) one."

The Saduth tale uses the archaic singular, and also the archaic word *alen*, in "I am alone": *Je-eri alen*. This archaic singular was otherwise used only for snake, and figuratively for sun, moon and occasionally tree. Thus any talk about a snake, however mundane, had this cast of the tale over it, a certain mysteriousness caused by grammatic necessity. When the Sorud called Tasman a snake, or Twar called his sons snakes, it was this archaic singular they had in mind.

About the Author

Heather Spears is a poet, author and artist. She won the Governor-General's Award for poetry in 1989 and the Pat Lowther Award twice. Part I of *Moonfall* was originally published in *Tesseracts 2* in 1987.

Heather Spears travels widely in Europe and the Middle East and lives in Copenhagen, Denmark.

Printed in Canada